my first
SEWING
MACHINE
BOOK

my first
SEWING MACHINE BOOK

learn to machine-sew
with confidence

- simple stitches
- helpful tips
- fun projects

Emma Hardy

CICO kidz

Published in 2014 by CICO Books
An imprint of Ryland Peters & Small
20–21 Jockey's Fields   341 E 116th St
London WC1R 4BW   New York, NY 10029
www.rylandpeters.com

10 9 8 7 6

A CIP catalog record for this book is available from
the Library of Congress and the British Library.

ISBN: 978-1-78249-101-9

Printed in China

Editor: Sarah Hoggett
Series consultant: Susan Akass
Designer: Barbara Zuñiga
Animal illustrator: Hannah George
Step illustrator: Rachel Boulton
Photographer: Debbie Patterson
Stylist: Emma Hardy

Contents

Introduction

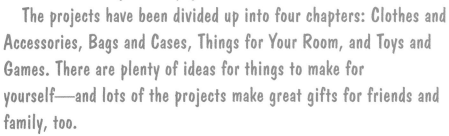

Once you have got your sewing machine, you will be eager to get going on it! This book will help you through the basics and give you lots of ideas for projects to stitch. There are 35 projects to make with a sewing machine, ranging from a simple lavender bag (page 88) and needle case (page 86) to a pretty rag doll (page 92) with a stylish outfit and matching shoes (page 95).

The projects have been divided up into four chapters: Clothes and Accessories, Bags and Cases, Things for Your Room, and Toys and Games. There are plenty of ideas for things to make for yourself—and lots of the projects make great gifts for friends and family, too.

All the projects are graded with one, two, or three smiley faces to show you how easy or difficult they are. Level one are great projects to start with, because they use only a few straight lines of stitching. There is more cutting and sewing for level two projects, but they are still quite easy to make. Level three projects are the hardest; try these when you have got the hang of your sewing machine and feel more confident.

Each project gives you a list of the tools and materials you will need, some of which you will probably have already. Lots of the projects need only small scraps of fabric; you could use bits left over from bigger projects if you have them or you could visit a fabric store and choose special fabrics for each project.

It is a good idea to put together a sewing kit (see Your Sewing Box, opposite) so that you will have them to hand while you sew. On pages 112–117, you can find all the stitches and techniques that you will need to know. Look out for the handy tips boxes, too, which tell you where to look for extra help with some of the techniques.

Your sewing box

We suggest you put together a sewing box that contains:

A pencil

A pen

A ruler

A tape measure

Squared paper (e.g. from a math book) for making patterns

Large sheets of paper such as newspaper or brown parcel paper

Thin paper for tracing templates

Scissors for cutting paper

Sharp scissors kept especially for cutting fabric (using them for paper will make them blunt)

Pinking shears

Small pointed embroidery scissors

Pins

Safety pins

Stitch ripper

Tailor's chalk

Needles, including some big ones with big eyes

A needle threader (this will save you a lot of time!)

Cotton threads and embroidery floss (thread) in different colors

Fiberfill (stuffing)

Cotton batting (wadding)

You will also need:

Fabrics—these are available in a huge range of colors and patterns. Often, small pieces (remnants) are sold very cheaply, so look out for those. Save old clothes that are too worn to pass on, and re-use the fabric—and always keep pieces of fabric left over from your sewing projects, as you never know when you might want a small piece!

Felt is great to use, as it does not fray. A selection of felt in different colors is a must and can often be bought in mixed packs from craft stores.

Buttons—again, these are available in a range of colors and sizes. Cut them off old clothing and store them in a glass jar ready to be used for your sewing projects.

Ribbons, braids, and rick-rack—available from sewing notion (haberdashery) stores. Look out for them on gifts and boxes of chocolates, too!

Project levels

Level 1

These are quick and easy projects.

Level 2

These projects are quite easy but take a little longer to complete.

Level 3

These projects use advanced techniques and may need help from an adult.

Chapter 1
Clothes and Accessories

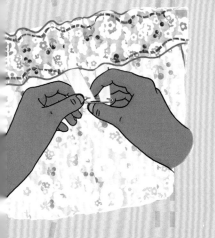

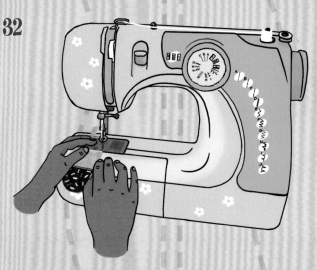

Pin-on popsicles

Pretty up a bag or jacket with an almost "good-enough-to-eat" popsicle (ice-lolly) brooch. Think about your favorite flavors and then choose your felt colors to match—pink for strawberry and raspberry, yellow for lemon or banana, bright green for lime, dark brown for chocolate. They are simple and quick to make, so why not make a few as gifts for friends and family?

You will need

Templates on page 118

5½ x 4 in. (14 x 10 cm) dark pink felt

3 x 3 in. (8 x 8 cm) light pink felt

2½ x 2½ in. (6 x 6 cm) dark brown felt

2½ x 1½ in. (6 x 4 cm) light brown felt

Contrasting thread for basting (tacking)

White sewing thread

Embroidery floss (thread) in pale blue, yellow, green, and pink

Small handful of polyester toy filling

Brooch pin

Paper for patterns

Pencil

Scissors

Pins

Embroidery and sewing needles

Sewing machine

1 Trace templates A, B, C, and the popsicle stick on page 118 and cut them out. Fold the dark pink felt in half, then pin shape C to it. Pin shape B to the pale pink felt, shape A to the dark brown felt, and the stick to the pale brown felt. Cut them all out neatly.

2 Pin the pale brown stick shape to the bottom edge of one of the dark pink shapes, making sure that at least ⅜ in. (1 cm) of the stick is on the pink felt. Thread a needle with sewing thread, baste (tack) the stick in place. Take out the pin. This will be the back of the popsicle.

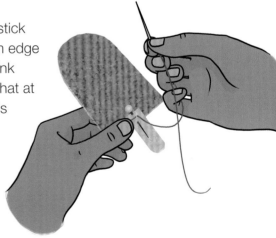

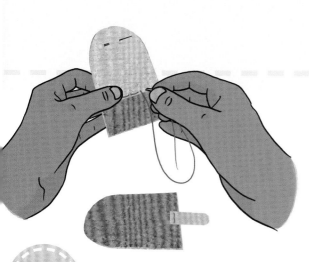

3 Now make the front of the popsicle. Pin the pale pink B shape to the top of the second dark pink C shape, lining up the edges. Baste along the bottom straight edge of B, then take out the pins. Machine stitch, then take out the basting stitches.

4 Pin and baste the dark brown A shape to the pale pink B shape, lining up the top edge neatly. You will now be sewing through three layers of felt, so it will be harder to sew. Take out the pins. Machine stitch along the bottom straight edge, then take out the basting stitches.

5 If you are making sprinkles (hundreds and thousands), take a length of embroidery floss (thread), tie a knot in one end, and thread the other end through the needle. Fold the brown felt forward slightly, away from the pale pink, so that you will be sewing through just one layer of felt. Starting from the back to the front, sew a few stitches randomly and finish on the back with a knot. Do this with the other flosses, making about two or three stitches in each color.

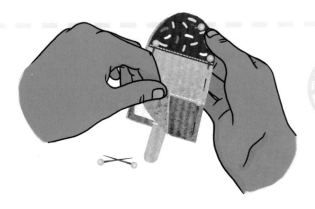

6 Put the back of the popsicle right side down on your table (the stick will be on top), then place a handful of toy filling on top, spreading it out evenly. Put the front of the popsicle, stripy side up, on top of this and pin it in place. Tuck inside any stuffing that shows around the edges, as you pin.

7 Baste all the way around the popsicle, then take out the pins. Machine stitch as close to the edge as you can. Always remember to start and finish machine stitching securely (see page 114). Take out the basting stitches.

8 Open the brooch pin and place it on the back of the popsicle, in the middle. You will see that the pin has several holes in the back. Thread a needle with sewing thread and knot the end. Push the needle into the back layer of felt, close to the first hole, and bring it up through the hole. Make several more stitches through the hole, stitching from both sides of the pin, then push the needle under the back layer of felt to the next hole and stitch that in the same way. Stitch through all the other holes in the brooch pin, and finish with a few stitches over and over in one place to secure the thread.

Summer skirt

Make yourself a skirt that no one else will have! Choose a pretty patterned fabric, and add a contrasting trim of rick-rack, if you like, though you can just miss out step 8 if you are keeping your skirt plain. The finished length of the skirt is 15⅜ in. (39 cm), but you can easily make it shorter by making the hem larger, or make it longer by using more fabric.

You will need

Cotton fabric, 20 in. (50 cm) by the width of the fabric—in this case, 45 in. (115 cm)

25 in. (63 cm) elastic, 1 in. (2.5 cm) wide—or long enough to fit around your waist plus 2 in. (5 cm)

45 in. (115 cm) rick-rack (optional)

Contrasting thread for basting (tacking)

Sewing threads to match the fabric and rick-rack

Pins

Sewing needle

Scissors

Tape measure

Sewing machine

Safety pin

1 If your fabric is too long, the easiest way to get the correct length is to rip it! Fabric will rip in straight lines. Make sure that the end of the fabric is straight, then measure the length you need (20 in./50 cm), make a small nick at the side with a pair of scissors, and rip it apart.

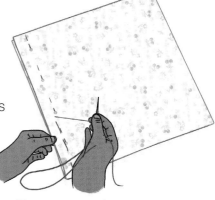

2 Fold the fabric in half, right sides together, so that the two short sides meet. Pin and baste (tack) along this edge, then take out the pins. Thread your sewing machine with thread to match the fabric, then machine stitch along this edge, stitching ⅝ in. (1.5 cm) from the edge. Always remember to start and finish machine stitching securely (see page 114). Take out the basting stitches. Ask an adult to help you press the seam open with an iron, then let the fabric cool completely.

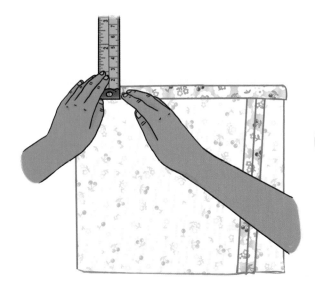

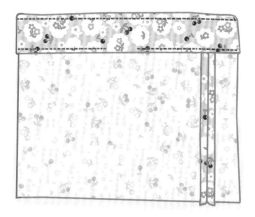

3 With the wrong side of the fabric facing out, fold down ⅜ in (1 cm) of fabric from the top edge all the way around the skirt. Keep checking the width with your tape measure. Press it over with your fingers and add a few pins to keep it in place if the fabric is very springy. Ask an adult to help you press along the fold with an iron, then let the fabric cool completely.

4 Turn the top edge over again by 1½ in. (4 cm) and pin and baste it in place. Take out the pins. Machine stitch around the top, close to the folded edge. Then stitch around the bottom edge of the folded-over fabric, stopping about 2½ in. (6 cm) before you get all the way round so that you have a gap in the stitching. Take out the basting stitches.

5 Fasten the safety pin to one end of the elastic and push it up through the gap and all the way through the channel that you have just made at the top of the skirt, gathering the skirt up as you go. When the elastic comes out of the other side, pin both ends together with the safety pin. Try the skirt on to make sure that the elastic isn't too tight or too loose; move the safety pin if you have to, to get a comfortable fit.

6 Overlap the ends of the elastic by about 1 in. (2.5 cm) (trim the ends if you need to) and pin and baste them together. Then take out the pin, pull the overlapped ends away from the skirt, and machine stitch. Use the reverse on the machine to stitch backward and forward a few times to make it really secure. Push the elastic inside the channel and machine stitch the gap closed.

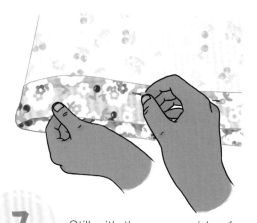

7 Still with the wrong side of the skirt facing out, fold the bottom edge up by ⅜ in. (1 cm) and ask an adult to help you press the fold with an iron. Fold the bottom edge up by another 2 in. (5 cm)—or more if you want your skirt to be shorter—pin, and baste in place. Take out the pins. Machine stitch all the way around, making sure you stitch at the top edge of the hem where the double fold is and keeping your stitch line nice and straight. Take out the basting stitches and turn the skirt right side out.

Try it on and take a TWIRL!

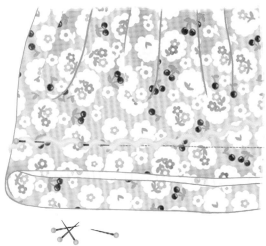

8 For a finishing touch, pin and baste rick-rack around the bottom of the skirt over the hem stitch line. Fold the end of the rick-rack under neatly. Take out the pins. Thread your sewing machine with thread to match the rick-rack and machine stitch it in place. Take out the basting stitches and ask an adult to help you press the skirt with an iron.

Felt slippers

These felt mouse slippers are so cute that you will never want to take them off! They can be made to fit any shoe size—simply cut out the front section of the slipper sole and draw around the back of your own foot to make the correct size. Felt can be slippy, so adding a non-slip sole will make them much safer to wear.

You will need

Templates on page 119

24 x 12 in. (60 x 30 cm) craft felt, ¼ in. (5 mm) thick

4-in. (10-cm) square of patterned fabric

Four black buttons for the eyes, about ⅝ in. (1.5 cm) in diameter

Two pink buttons for the noses, about ¾ in. (2 cm) in diameter

10 in. (24 cm) thin ribbon

Non-slip fabric for the soles

Contrasting thread for basting (tacking)

Black sewing thread and thread to match the felt

Scrap paper and pencil

Pins

Sewing needle

Sewing machine

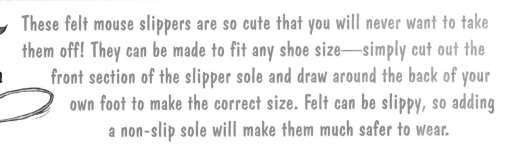

1 Trace the templates on page 119 onto scrap paper and cut them out. Pin the paper slipper top and outer ear patterns onto the felt and cut out one top and two outer ears for each slipper. Take out the pins and remove the patterns.

2 Place the paper slipper top on paper, place your foot on it, and then draw around the back of your foot to make a pattern the correct size for the slipper base. Cut out the pattern, then pin it to the felt and cut out two slipper soles. Take out the pins and remove the paper pattern.

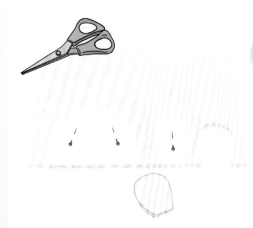

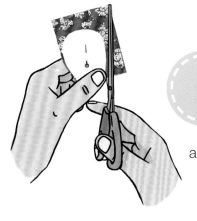

3 Pin the paper inner ear pattern to the patterned fabric and cut out four inner ear shapes—two for each slipper. Take out the pins and remove the paper pattern.

4 Pin the inner ears onto the felt ears, matching the straight edges. Baste (tack) them in place, then take out the pins. Pin two ears onto one of the slipper tops, angling them slightly so that they point outward at a jaunty angle, and baste them in place. Take out the pins and machine stitch the ears in place, stitching as close to the base of the ear as you can. Always remember to start and finish machine stitching securely (see page 114). Take out the basting stitches. Repeat, using the other ears and slipper top.

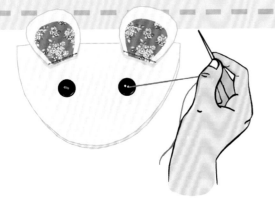

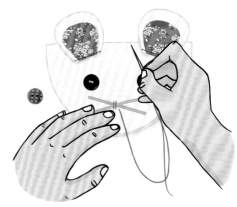

5 Using the needle and black thread, stitch two black button eyes (see page 117) onto each slipper top, starting and finishing with a few small stitches on the back of the slipper top so that the buttons will be secure.

6 Cut the ribbon into four pieces 2½ in. (6 cm) long. Lay two lengths of ribbon on a slipper top in a cross shape to make the whiskers. Sew a few small stitches where they cross and then stitch a pink button over the top of the cross to make the nose. Again, finish with few small stitches on the wrong side. Repeat to make whiskers and a nose on the other slipper top.

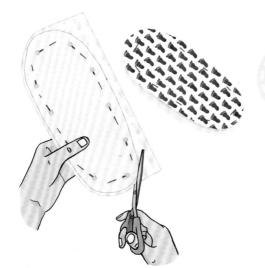

7 Pin the soles of the slippers onto the wrong side of the non-slip fabric (the smooth side) and cut out. Baste the fabrics together, removing the pins as you go, and then machine stitch all the way around both of them to make non-slip soles, stitching about ¼ in. (5 mm) from the outer edge. Remove the basting stitches.

8 Pin the slipper tops to the soles, bending the tops so that they fit along the edge of the base and form a foot shape. Baste them together, removing the pins as you go. Put the zipper foot on your sewing machine and carefully machine stitch the tops to the soles, being careful not to let the needle run off the felt. Take out the basting stitches.

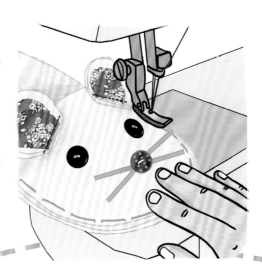

Animal ears

These cute bunny ears are fun to make as well as fun to wear. Stitch a pair of ears and fasten them onto a store-bought headband. Felt is great to use, as it is very easy to cut—and it doesn't fray, so you won't need to hem it.

You will need

Template on page 120

14 x 9 in. (36 x 22 cm) felt for outer ears

4 x 6 in. (10 x 15 cm) patterned fabric for inner ears

4 x 6 in. (10 x 15 cm) fusible bonding web

Contrasting thread for basting (tacking)

Sewing threads to match the felt and the patterned fabric

Polyester toy filling

Plastic headband

Tracing paper, scrap paper, and pencil (optional)

Pins

Scissors

Clean dish towel

Sewing needle

Sewing machine

1 Photocopy the templates on page 120 or trace them onto scrap paper and cut them out. You will have two paper shapes—a big shape for the outer ear and a small shape for the inner ear. Fold the felt in half and pin the big paper shape to it. (Pin it close to the edge so that you leave room to cut out another pair of ears.) Cut it out, then take out the pins and pin the same paper shape to what's left of the felt. Cut around the paper shape once more, so that you have four ear shapes all the same size.

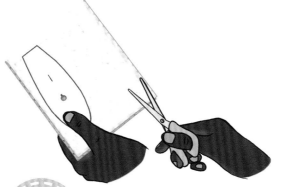

2 Place the fusible bonding web rough side down on the wrong side of the patterned fabric. Ask an adult to help you press it with an iron: the heat of the iron will make the bonding web stick to the fabric. Fold the fabric in half, pin the inner ear paper shape to it, and cut around the paper. You only need two inner ear shapes.

3 Peel the backing paper off both pieces of patterned fabric and place each one on a felt ear; the straight edge of the patterned fabric should line up with the straight edge of the felt. Cover with a clean dish towel, then ask an adult to help you press the fabrics so that they stick together. Let them cool down a little before you pick up the fabric pieces.

4 Thread your sewing machine with the thread that matches the patterned fabric and machine stitch around the edge of the inner ear. You can miss this step out if you find it a little fiddly, as the bonding web will hold the fabric in place, but sewing it will help to stop the fabric from coming away from the felt.

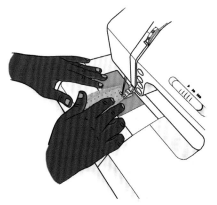

5 Take one piece of felt with a patterned inner ear and one plain piece of felt. Pin them together, with the inner ear piece on top. Baste (tack) them together, leaving the bottom edge open. Remove the pins as you sew. Thread your sewing machine with thread that matches the felt, then machine stitch around the felt ear, slowly and carefully, sewing about ¼ in. (5 mm) from the edge. Remove the basting stitches. Repeat with the other pair of ears.

6 Push small pieces of toy filling inside the ears, using the blunt end of a pencil to help you push it down to the tip. They need to be padded but not too fat. You don't need any padding at the bottom of the ear.

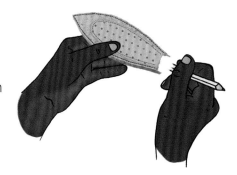

Get ready for a **FANCY-DRESS** party

7 Fold the bottom straight edge of the ears to the back by about ¾ in. (2 cm) and pin it in place to make a channel. Push the headband through this. If it fits snugly, then slip the ear off the headband again, baste, take out the pins, and machine stitch in place. If the channel is too tight or too loose, then alter the position of the pins before you baste and stitch along the ear in the correct place. Stitch both ears in this way and then push them onto the headband to finish.

Felt collar

Is your outfit missing a certain something? Jazz it up with this cute collar! To make a simpler collar that looks just as lovely, miss off the rick-rack or add beads or buttons for decoration.

You will need

Templates on page 118

8-in. (20-cm) square of cream felt

7-in. (18-cm) square of pink felt

20 in. (50 cm) rick-rack braid

24 in. (60 cm) ribbon to match the rick-rack

Contrasting thread for basting (tacking)

Thread to match the pink felt and rick-rack

Scrap paper and pencil

Scissors

Pins

Sewing needle

Sewing machine

1 Trace the templates on page 118 onto scrap paper and cut them out. Fold the cream felt and the pink felt in half. Pin the large collar shape to the cream felt and the small collar shape to the pink felt and cut around the patterns; you will have two collars in each color.

2 Pin the small paper collar pattern onto one of the cream felt collar shapes, matching up the inside edges. Using a pencil or tailor's chalk, draw around the outside edge of the pattern. Unpin the template. Flip the second cream collar piece over, then pin the small paper pattern to it and draw around it.

3 Cut the rick-rack braid in half. Pin one piece of rick-rack along each of the lines you drew in step 2, folding the ends under neatly. Baste (tack) along the rick-rack, removing the pins as you go. Using thread that matches the rick-rack, machine stitch the rick-rack in place, sewing slowly along the middle of the rick-rack so that you get the curve right. Always remember to start and finish machine stitching securely (see page 114). Take out the basting stitches.

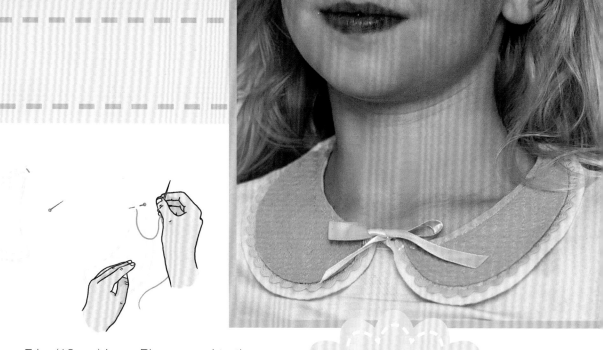

4

Cut a piece of ribbon 7 in. (18 cm) long. Pin one end to the back point of each cream felt collar (the end that is more pointy), on the wrong side, overlapping the ribbon on the felt by about ⅝ in. (1.5 cm). Baste the ribbon in place, then take out the pins. Machine stitch, using the reverse on the machine to stitch backward and forward a few times, which will secure the ribbon. Take out the basting stitches.

TIP

For tips on how to sew on a ribbon without basting first, see page 116.

5

Cut the remaining ribbon in half. Pin one end of each piece to the front point of each cream collar, on the wrong side. Make sure that the ribbon is pinned so that the end is about ⅝ in. (1.5 cm) beyond the stitching for the rick-rack. Baste it in place. Take out the pins and machine stitch, again stitching backward and forward a few times to hold the ribbon securely. The stitching will be covered over by the pink collar in the next stage.

6

Pin the pink collars onto the cream collars, just inside the rick-rack, matching up the inside edges. Baste along the inside edge, removing the pins as you go. Using pink thread, machine stitch the pink collars in place along the inside edge, stitching close to the edge. Then take out the basting stitches. To wear the collar, simply place it around your neck and tie the ribbons in a neat bow at the front.

Cozy scarf

Wrap up warm with a snuggly scarf that you have made yourself. We used soft fleece fabric, which is available in a huge range of colors, with a pretty patterned fabric as the backing. The ends of the scarf are folded over to make handy pockets.

You will need

7½ x 58 in. (19 x 145 cm) fleece fabric (see page 112 for tips about cutting out rectangles of fabric)

7½ x 58 in. (19 x 145 cm) patterned fabric

Contrasting thread for basting (tacking)

Sewing thread to match the fleece fabric

Two buttons (optional)

Pins

Sewing needle

Tailor's chalk

Scissors

Sewing machine

1 Lay the fleece fabric right side up on the table. Put the patterned fabric on top of it, right side down, matching up the edges. Smooth out the fabrics so that there are no creases. Pin all the way around the edge through both layers. Baste (tack) all the way around, taking out the pins as you go.

2 Make two marks with tailor's chalk about 4 in. (10 cm) apart in the middle of one long side. These will show you where to begin and end stitching, so that you remember to leave a gap for turning the scarf right side out. Start at one mark and machine stitch around the fabric to the other mark, stitching ⅝ in. (1.5 cm) from the edge. Remember to start and finish machine stitching securely (see page 114).

3 Snip off the corners at an angle, making sure that you do not cut into the stitching. This will give a neater finish to the scarf. Turn the scarf the right way out by pushing it through the gap in the stitching.

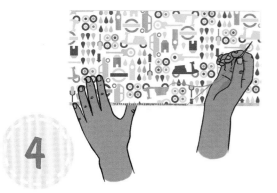

4

Thread a needle, then turn the seam allowance inside at the opening and slipstitch (see page 113) the opening closed. Start and finish with a few small stitches to secure the thread.

5

Turn the ends over to the patterned side of the scarf by 6 in. (15 cm) and pin down the sides to make the fleece pockets. Baste along the edges, removing the pins as you go, and then machine stitch the sides in place, stitching as close as you can to the edges of the fabric. Remove the basting stitches.

6

If you wish, for decoration, hand stitch a button onto the front of each pocket (see page 117). We used buttons covered in the same fabric as the scarf; you can buy kits for these at craft shops. Slip a piece of cardboard into the pocket when you sew the button on, to stop you from stitching the pocket closed!

Appliquéd t-shirt

Can't find a thing to wear? This cool T-shirt will definitely get you noticed. Appliqué is a great way of decorating a plain top and you can choose any fabric that you like for your design. Use the zig-zag stitch on your sewing machine so that the star shape will be firmly stitched in place.

You will need

10-in. (25-cm) square of fusible bonding web

12-in. (30-cm) square of fabric for the appliqué

Template on page 121

T-shirt

Sewing thread to match the appliqué fabric

Scrap paper and pencil

Pins

Scissors

Clean dish towel

Sewing machine

1 Place the fusible bonding web rough side down on the wrong side of the fabric you are using for the appliqué. Ask an adult to help you press the bonding web with an iron, so that it sticks to the fabric. The fabric may be hot after ironing, so let it cool for a moment before you pick it up.

2 Trace the template on page 121 onto scrap paper and cut out the star shape. Pin it onto the bonding web side of the fabric and draw around it. Cut the star out carefully. The best way to do this is always to cut inward along the straight edges of the points, toward the center of the star. Take out the pins.

3 Lay the T-shirt on an ironing board, making sure that it is nice and flat. Peel the backing paper off the fabric star and place the star on the middle of the T-shirt front. Lay a clean dish towel over the star and ask an adult to help you press it with an iron, so that the star sticks to the T-shirt. Again, leave the T-shirt to cool before you pick it up.

STAR quality!

4 Change the stitch setting on your machine to a zig-zag stitch. Place the T-shirt on the sewing machine, and zig-zag stitch around the edges of the star. When you get to a corner, make sure that the needle is down in the fabric (if it is not, use the wheel at the side of the machine to lower it), then lift the presser foot and turn the fabric, ready to stitch the next side; lower the presser foot again and carry on stitching. Trim the threads.

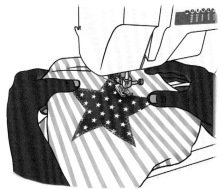

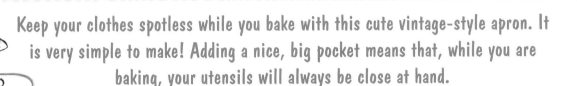

Cook's apron

Keep your clothes spotless while you bake with this cute vintage-style apron. It is very simple to make! Adding a nice, big pocket means that, while you are baking, your utensils will always be close at hand.

You will need

16 x 14 in. (40 x 35 cm) fabric for the apron (see page 112 for tips about cutting out rectangles of fabric)

8 x 6 in. (20 x 15 cm) fabric for the pocket

48 in. (120 cm) wide ribbon, about 2 in. (5 cm) wide

Contrasting thread for basting (tacking)

Sewing thread to match the fabric

Pinking shears

Pins

Sewing machine

Ruler or tape measure

Tailor's chalk

1 Cut out a rectangle of newspaper or brown paper that measures 15 x 13½ in. (38 x 34 cm). This will be a pattern for the apron. Cut another one that measures 7½ x 5½ in. (19 x 14 cm) for the pocket. Pin these patterns to the two fabrics and cut around them using pinking shears.

2 Put the apron fabric right side down on the table. Fold each edge over to the wrong side by ⅝ in. (1.5 cm) and pin the edges in place. Baste (tack) around all four sides, taking out the pins as you go. Thread your machine with thread to match the fabric and machine stitch around all four sides of the fabric, sewing in the middle of the folded-over edge. Remember to start and finish machine stitching securely (see page 114). Take out the basting stitches.

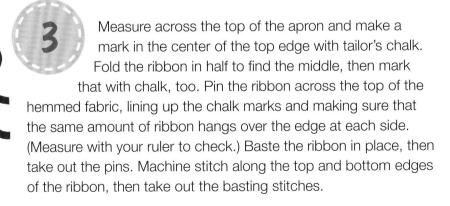

3 Measure across the top of the apron and make a mark in the center of the top edge with tailor's chalk. Fold the ribbon in half to find the middle, then mark that with chalk, too. Pin the ribbon across the top of the hemmed fabric, lining up the chalk marks and making sure that the same amount of ribbon hangs over the edge at each side. (Measure with your ruler to check.) Baste the ribbon in place, then take out the pins. Machine stitch along the top and bottom edges of the ribbon, then take out the basting stitches.

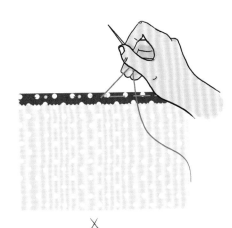

4 Fold the top edge of the pocket fabric over to the wrong side by ⅝ in. (1.5 cm). Pin it in place, then baste, removing the pins as you go. Machine stitch, sewing ⅜ in. (1 cm) from the folded edge. Take out the basting stitches.

Every COOK needs an apron!

5 Lay the apron on the table and place the pocket on top of it, both right side up. Using the tape measure, make sure that the pocket is 3 in. (8 cm) from the bottom edge of the apron and the same distance from each side. Pin around the side and bottom edges of the pocket, then baste around the same three sides, leaving the top edge open and removing the pins as you stitch. Machine stitch the pocket in place, stitching close to the edge, then take out the basting stitches. Your apron will look even nicer if you ask an adult to help you press it with an iron when you have finished.

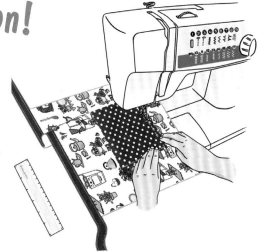

Fabric belt

Accessorize your outfit with a pretty belt. Coordinate it with your favorite dress or team it with a plain T-shirt and jeans. Choose colorful ribbons and add bright wooden beads for extra decoration. The finished belt is 20 in. (51 cm) long, plus the ribbons.

You will need

22 x 4½ in. (56 x 11 cm) fabric (see page 112 for tips about cutting out rectangles of fabric)

22 in. (56 cm) pink ribbon, 1 in. (2.5 cm) wide

22 in. (56 cm) patterned ribbon, ⅜ in. (1 cm) wide

22 in. (56 cm) thin ribbon

12 colored beads, with holes big enough for the thin ribbon to go through them

Contrasting thread for basting (tacking)

Sewing thread to match the patterned ribbon

Pins

Sewing needle

Large safety pin

Scissors

Sewing machine

Sticky tape

1 Fold the fabric in half, with right sides together, and pin along the long side. Baste (tack) along the long side, removing the pins as you go. Machine stitch, stitching ⅜ in. (1 cm) from the edge and leaving the short ends open. Always remember to start and finish machine stitching securely (see page 114).

2 Fasten the safety pin through one end of the tube and push it through the inside to the other end to turn the fabric the right way out. Take the safety pin off.

3 Squash the tube so that the seam runs along the middle and ask an adult to help you press it flat with an iron.

4 Take the pink ribbon and pin it down the middle of the fabric. Baste it in place, taking the pins out as you go, and then machine stitch it in place, stitching down the middle of the ribbon.

5

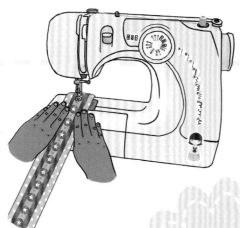

Pin the patterned ribbon onto the middle of the pink ribbon. Baste it in place, taking the pins out as you go, and then machine stitch it in place, stitching down the middle of the ribbon.

TIP

For tips on how to sew on a ribbon without basting first, see page 116.

A fun, FUNKY belt!

6 Fold both short ends of the strip over to the wrong side by 1 in. (2.5 cm) and ask an adult to help you press them with an iron. Cut the thin ribbon in half. Fold one piece in half and pin the folded end onto one end of the belt. Pin it to the wrong side on the fold that you've just pressed. Baste it and take out the pin. Repeat with the second piece of ribbon at the other end of the belt. Machine stitch across both ends of the belt, ⅝ in. (1.5 cm) from the end, making sure that you stitch across the ribbon, then take out all the basting stitches.

7 Thread three beads onto each ribbon and tie a knot in the end of each ribbon to hold the beads in place. If the beads are difficult to thread, wrap a small piece of sticky tape tightly around the end of each ribbon to make them stiff enough to push through the holes. Pull the tape off before you tie the knot.

Hair bows

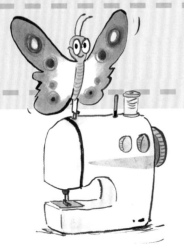

Make these pretty hair bows to coordinate with an outfit or, with pins stitched onto the back instead of clips, they make great brooches to brighten up a jacket, or to give as gifts. They are a clever way of using up scraps of fabric, too.

You will need

11 x 8 in. (28 x 21 cm) fabric (see page 112 for tips about cutting out rectangles of fabric)

Contrasting thread for basting (tacking)

Sewing thread to match the fabric

Polyester toy filling

Hair clip

Squared paper, ruler, and pencil

Pins

Sewing needle

Tailor's chalk

Sewing machine

1 Measure and draw a 7-in. (18-cm) square on squared paper and cut it out. Pin the paper square onto the fabric and cut around it, so that you have a fabric square. Take out the pins.

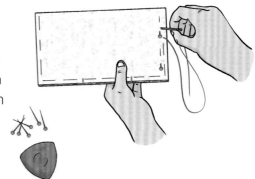

2 Fold the fabric in half, with the right sides together. Pin along the three open sides. Baste (tack) along them, taking out the pins as you go. Make two marks with tailor's chalk about 2 in. (5 cm) apart along the long side; these will show you where to begin and end stitching. Starting at one cross, machine stitch all the way round to the other cross, stitching about ⅝ in. (1.5 cm) from the edge of the fabric. Remember to start and finish machine stitching securely (see page 114).

Clip-on BOWS!

3 Take out the basting stitches and trim the corners at an angle, taking care not to cut into the stitching. Turn the fabric the right way out by pushing it through the gap in the stitching. Push the corners out, using the blunt end of a pencil.

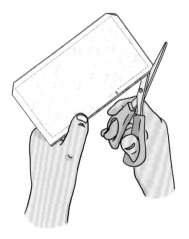

4 Push small pieces of toy filling inside the fabric to make it padded, but not too fat. Thread a needle, then turn the seam allowance inside at the opening and slipstitch (see page 113) the opening closed. Start and finish with a few small stitches to secure the thread.

5 Measure and draw a 3½-in. (9-cm) square on squared paper and cut it out. Pin it onto the remaining fabric, draw around it, and cut out the fabric square, just as you did in step 1. Take out the pins.

6 Fold the fabric square in half, with right sides together. Pin and baste along the long side only, taking out the pins as you go. Machine stitch along this side and then take out the basting stitches. Trim the seam allowance to about ¼ in. (5 mm) wide. Turn the fabric the right way out.

7 Squash the tube flat with the seam running along the middle, then turn it over so that the seam is underneath. Fold down the top half of the fabric, bringing the raw ends together. Pin and baste the ends together and remove the pins. Machine stitch across the ends, then take out the basting stitches.

8 Turn the fabric ring the other way out (so that the seams are on the inside). Push the padded rectangle through the tube until the same amount sticks out on both sides to make a bow. Make sure that none of the seam is showing on the front.

9 Hand stitch a hair clip onto the back of the bow, sewing it across the seam. Make sure you sew it securely in place, with lots of stitches crossing over the bar all along the back of the clip.

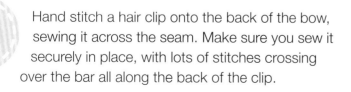

Chapter 2
Bags and Cases

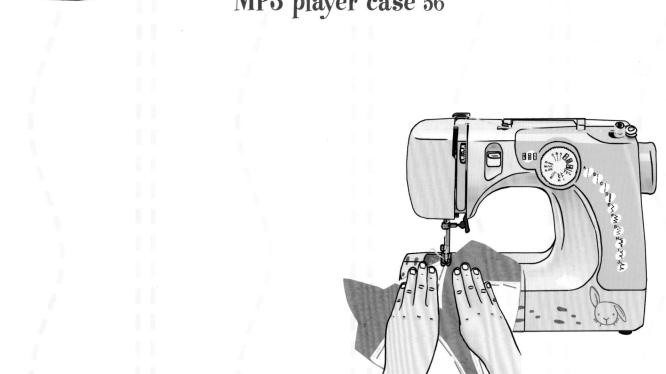

Drawstring bags

Keep your room looking pretty and organized with these easy-to-make drawstring bags, which are great for storing toys, shoes, or toiletries. The bags hang up by their ribbons, with the wooden beads making a stylish finishing touch.

You will need

At least 27½ x 18 in. (70 x 45 cm) fabric

34 in. (85 cm) ribbon, ⅜ in. (1 cm) wide

Sewing thread to match the fabric

Contrasting thread for basting (tacking)

Two colored beads

Newspaper or brown wrapping paper for pattern

Scissors

Pins

Tape measure

Pencil

Sewing machine

Sewing needle

Safety pin

Sticky tape

1 If your fabric needs to be cut to size, use a piece of newspaper or brown wrapping paper to cut out a 27½ x 18-in. (70 x 45-cm) rectangle of paper. (See page 112 for tips on cutting rectangles.) Pin the paper pattern to the fabric and cut it out.

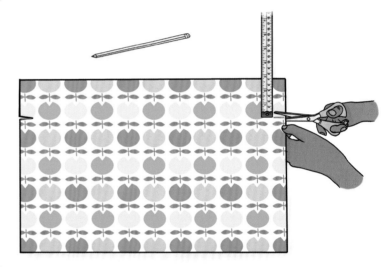

2 Lay the fabric on the table. Using the tape measure and pencil, measure 2¾ in. (7 cm) down from the top left corner and then draw a line inward, ⅝ in. (1.5 cm) from the side. Snip along this line. Do the same at the top right corner.

3 Thread your sewing machine with thread to match the fabric. Fold the small flap above the snip over to the wrong side and pin it.

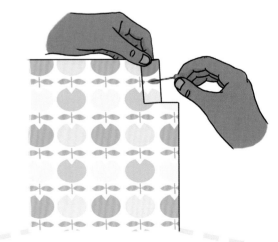

4 Put the flap under the sewing machine foot and wind the needle down by hand so it is through the fabric—this will hold the flap in place so that you can take the pin out before you stitch. Stitch ⅜ in. (1 cm) from the folded edge. You will not need to baste (tack) this as it is so small. Repeat for the other flap.

Perfect for a TIDY bedroom

5 With the wrong side of the fabric facing up, fold the top edge over by ⅜ in. (1 cm), creasing it with your fingers and maybe adding a few pins. Ask an adult to help you press it with an iron, then let the fabric cool and take out the pins.

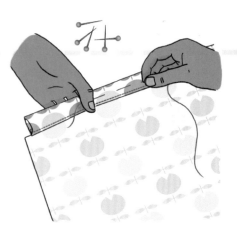

6 Fold the top over again by 1¼ in. (3 cm), so that the bottom edge lines up with the snip that you made on either side of the fabric. Pin and baste this in place to make the channel across the top of the bag. Take out the pins and machine stitch about ¼ in. (5 mm) from the bottom folded edge. Always remember to start and finish machine stitching securely (see page 114). Take out the basting stitches.

7 With right sides together, fold the fabric in half, lining up the edges neatly. Pin and baste along the side edge and across the bottom. Take out the pins. Machine stitch in place up to the bottom edge of the channel, stitching ⅝ in. (1.5 cm) from the edge. Take out the basting stitches.

8 Turn the bag right side out. Ask an adult to help you press the bag with an iron. Fasten the safety pin to one end of the ribbon. Push the safety pin all the way through the channel at the top of the bag until it comes out of the other side. Take the safety pin off the ribbon.

9 Hold the two ends of the ribbon together and wind a small piece of sticky tape tightly around them to make a firm point that will thread through the beads. Thread on both beads, pull off the sticky tape, and tie the ends of the ribbon with a double knot to finish.

Bobble-trim purse

If you want to make your own clothes, you will have to learn to sew in zippers and this pretty, multi-purpose purse is a really good place to start. To sew in a zipper is surprisingly easy, but make sure that your sewing machine has a zipper foot, which will enable you to stitch along the zipper neatly.

You will need

At least 9 x 10 in. (23 x 26 cm) floral fabric

At least 9 x 7 in (23 x 18 cm) gingham fabric

18 in. (46 cm) bobble trim

8-in. (20-cm) zipper

7 in. (18 cm) ribbon

Contrasting thread for basting (tacking)

Sewing thread to match the fabric

Squared paper

Pencil and ruler

Tape measure

Scissors

Pins

Sewing needle

Sewing machine with a zipper foot

1 If your fabric needs to be cut to size, use squared paper—for example, from a math book—to cut out one 9 x 10-in. (23 x 26-cm) rectangle and one 9 x 7-in. (23 x 18-cm) rectangle. (See page 112 for tips on cutting out squares and rectangles). Use these as patterns to cut out the floral fabric and gingham fabric pieces.

2 Fold the floral fabric in half and cut along the fold so that you have two rectangles measuring 9 x 5 in. (23 x 13 cm). Do the same with the gingham fabric so that you have two rectangles measuring 9 x 3½ in. (23 x 9 cm). With right sides together, place a gingham piece along the top of a floral piece, pin them together, and baste (tack) along the top edge. Take out the pins. Machine stitch along the basted edge, ⅝ in. (1.5 cm) from the edge, remembering to start and finish machine stitching securely (see page 114), then take out the basting stitches. Repeat with the other gingham and floral fabric rectangles. Ask an adult to help you press the seam open.

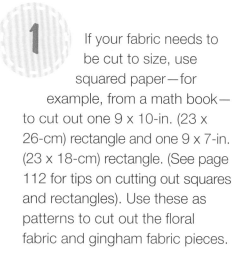

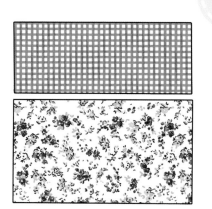

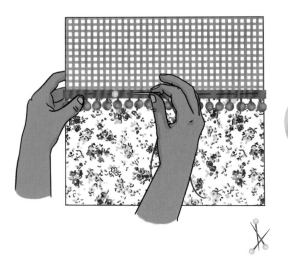

3 Cut the bobble trim in half. Pin and baste the flat part of the bobble trim along the join between the fabrics (on the right side), then take out the pins. Machine stitch it in place, stitching along the flat part of the bobble trim. Repeat with the other piece of bobble trim and the other piece of fabric, then take out all the basting stitches.

4 Place one of the pieces of fabric right side up on the table, with the gingham at the top. Put the zipper right side down along the top edge of the fabric, lining up the edge of the zipper with the edge of the fabric. Pin and baste it in place, then take out the pins. Put the zipper foot on the sewing machine and machine stitch along the zipper.

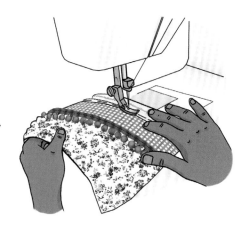

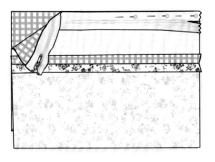

5 Lay the other piece of fabric right side up on the table, with the gingham at the top. Put the fabric with the zipper attached to it right side down on top, so that the edge of the other side of the zipper lines up with the top edge of the fabric. Pin, baste, and machine stitch the zipper to the fabric in the same way as before, then take out all the basting stitches.

6 To sew the purse up, open the zipper halfway along (to give you a gap to turn the purse through) and then, with right sides together, pin the two halves together, matching up the corners exactly. Baste around the three sides, then take out the pins. Change the foot on the sewing machine back to the regular one and machine stitch along all three sides, sewing ⅝ in. (1.5 cm) from the edge. Take out the basting stitches.

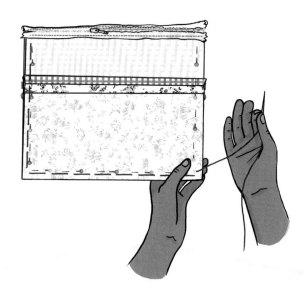

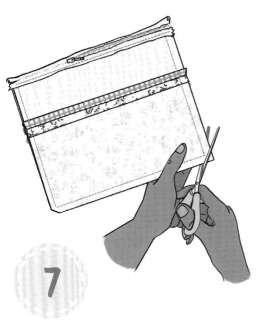

7

With a sharp pair of scissors, cut diagonally across the bottom corners, taking care not to cut through the stitching. This will help the corners to lie smoothly.

ZIP UP your treasures

8 Turn the purse right side out and push the corners out neatly, using a blunt pencil. Take the length of ribbon and fold it in half. Push the looped end through the hole in the zipper pull. Thread the ends of the ribbon back through the loop and pull it to tighten it. The ribbon will help you to open and close the zipper. Ask an adult to help you press the purse with an iron.

Laundry bag

Why not make your own pretty laundry bag for your dirty clothes? If you love dinosaurs, then this fabric is perfect—we fastened a plastic dinosaur toy onto the ends of the ribbon to continue the dinosaur theme. Or you could choose a fabric with a different theme and tie a small toy or colorful beads onto the ends of the ribbons instead.

You will need

48 in. (120 cm) patterned fabric, 44 in. (112 cm) wide

5 x 44 in. (12 x 112 cm) polka-dot fabric

90 in. (230 cm) cotton tape or ribbon

Contrasting thread for basting (tacking)

Sewing thread to match the fabric

Template on page 120

Plastic dinosaur/beads/toy with hanging ring

Newspaper or brown wrapping paper for pattern

Pencil and ruler

Scissors

Pins

Sewing needle

Sewing machine

Safety pin

1 Draw a 22 x 40-in. (55 x 102-cm) and a 5 x 40-in. (12 x 102-cm) rectangle on newspaper or brown wrapping paper and cut them out. (See page 112 for tips on cutting rectangles.) Pin the large rectangle to the patterned fabric and cut it out. Pin the small rectangle to the polka-dot fabric and cut that out.

2 Take the polka-dot fabric and lay it along the top of the patterned fabric, with right sides together. Pin and baste (tack) along the top edge. Take out the pins. Machine stitch, sewing ⅝ in. (1.5 cm) from the edge. Always remember to start and finish machine stitching securely (see page 114). Take out the basting stitches. Ask an adult to help you press the seam open.

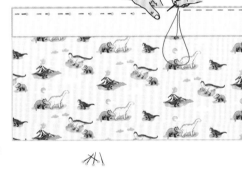

3 Open the fabric out. Measure 8¾ in. (21 cm) down from the top corner and cut a snip ⅝ in. (1.5 cm) long. Do the same along the other side of the fabric.

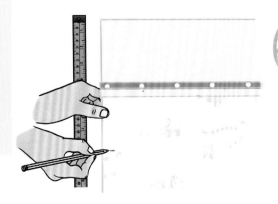

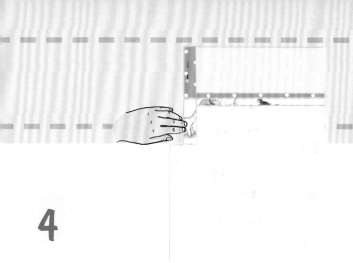

4

Fold the fabric above the snip over to the wrong side by ⅝ in. (1.5 cm) and pin and baste it in place. Stitch ⅜ in. (1 cm) from the folded edge. Repeat for the other flap. Remove the basting stitches.

Fold the top edge over by ⅜ in. (1 cm) and ask an adult to help you press it with an iron.

6

Fold the top over again so that the seam between the two fabrics runs across the top edge. Pin and baste along the bottom folded edge. Take out the pins. Machine stitch ⅜ in. (1 cm) from the bottom edge. Use a ruler and tailor's chalk to draw a line 1 in. (2.5 cm) above this stitching and then machine stitch along it. This will make a channel for the ribbon. Take out the basting stitches.

7

Fold the fabric in half with right sides together and pin and baste the side edges together. Take out the pins. Machine stitch along the sides to the bottom of the channel, stitching ⅝ in. (1.5 cm) from the edge. Take out the basting stitches.

8 Ask an adult to photocopy the base template on page 120 using the 200% zoom button on the photocopier, then cut out the shape. Pin the paper circle to the remaining patterned fabric and cut it out. Take off the paper. The fabric circle will be the base of the bag.

9 With right sides together, pin and baste the base to the bottom edge of the bag. Take out the pins. Machine stitch in place, sewing ⅜ in. (1 cm) from the edge, working slowly and carefully turning the fabric as you go. Take out the basting stitches.

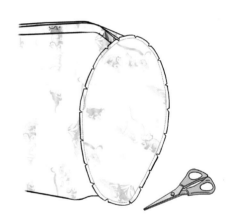

10 Snip small V-shapes into the fabric all the way around the base seam, being very careful not to snip into the stitching.

11 Turn the bag the right way out, then ask an adult to help you press it. Fasten the safety pin to one end of the ribbon and use this to thread the ribbon through the bottom channel around the top of the bag. When the safety pin comes through the other side of the bag, take it off and knot the ends of the ribbon together. Alternatively, thread a plastic toy or some beads onto the ribbon and then knot or sew the ends together.

Fox bag

Everyone will comment when they see this brightly colored fox bag over your shoulder! The bag is simple to make but it will need some very neat stitching, so practice sewing on scrap felt first.

You will need

Templates on page 122

22 x 10 in. (50 x 25 cm) orange felt

11 x 8 in. (30 x 20 cm) white felt

4-in. (10-cm) square of black felt

3-in. (8-cm) square of green felt

2-in. (5-cm) square of pink felt

32 in. (80 cm) ribbon

Contrasting thread for basting (tacking)

Sewing thread in white and black

Button

Paper for pattern

Pencil

Scissors

Pins

Sewing needle

Sewing machine

1 Trace the templates on page 122 onto paper and cut them out. Fold the orange felt in half and cut it into two pieces. Fold one piece in half again, pin pattern A to it (dotted line along fold) and cut out one head. Repeat with the other piece of orange felt. Fold the white felt in half, pin pattern B to it, and cut out. Cut one piece C from white felt for the top of the head, two eyes and a nose from black felt, one large green felt flower, and one small pink felt flower. Take off the paper patterns.

2 Pin the two white B shapes to one orange head shape; the template shows where they should go. Baste (tack) them in place around the curved inside edges. Pin and baste piece C to the top, stitching around all three sides. Take out the pins.

3 Thread your machine with white thread. Machine stitch the white felt pieces in place, stitching along the edges that you basted in step 2. Always remember to start and finish machine stitching securely (see page 114). Take out the basting stitches.

4 Pin the black felt eyes onto the face (the template shows where they should go) and baste them in place. Take out the pins. Thread your machine with black thread and machine stitch around the circular part (leave the eyelashes free). Take out the basting stitches.

5 The other orange head shape will be the back of the bag. Pin and baste one end of the ribbon to the top of each ear, making sure that the end of the ribbon is abc 2 in. (5 cm) below the tip of the ear. Machine stitch acros the ribbon ends, stitching about ¾ in. (2 cm) down the ea Take out the basting stitches.

6 Put the front of the bag onto the back, lining up the edges exactly. Pin them together. Starting at the tip of one ear and working down the face and up the other side to the tip of the other ear, baste them together, leaving the inner parts of the ears and the top of the head unstitched, so that the bag is open at the top. Take out the pins. Thread your machine with white thread. Following your basting stitches, machine stitch the front and back together, sewing as close to the edge as you can. Go slowly so that you don't run off the felt. Take out the basting stitches.

7 Thread your machine with black thread. Pin and then baste the felt nose in place, then take out the pins. Machine stitch across the nose. Take out the basting stitches.

Fabulous MISS FOX bag!

8 Thread a needle with thread to match your button, pull it through so that it is double, and knot the ends together. From the inside of the ear, push your needle up through the center of the flowers and then through one of the holes in the button. Take the needle back through another of the holes. Keep stitching up and down through the flower and button until they are securely stitched on. Make sure you don't stitch through to the back of the bag! Finish with a few stitches over and over on the back.

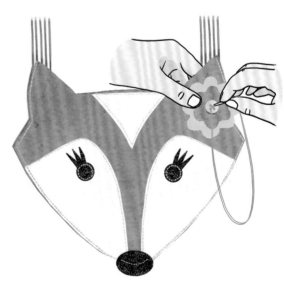

Laptop case

Make sure your laptop or tablet stays safe from knocks and bumps with this padded case! You can make it bright and fun with your own choice of fabric, but you will need to do a bit of careful measuring to work out how much fabric you need.

You will need

Patterned fabric

Gingham fabric

Cotton batting (wadding)

Ribbon ⅝ in. (1.5 cm) wide and twice the length of your laptop plus about 22 in. (55 cm)

Contrasting thread for basting (tacking)

Sewing thread to match the fabric and the ribbon

Four buttons (optional)

Scrap paper, ruler, and pencil or tailor's chalk (optional)

Pins

Scissors

Sewing needle

Sewing machine

1 Start with some math to work out how much fabric you need. First, measure the long side of your laptop or tablet. Add 3 in. (8 cm) to this measurement and write it down. Now measure the short side. Add 1 in. (2.5 cm) to this measurement, then double it and write it down. Check the measurements and your math again to make sure they're right!

2 Either cut out a rectangle of paper (see page 112) using the measurements you have just worked out and use it as a pattern for all three fabrics or measure directly onto the gingham—the squares in the fabric will help you cut straight lines and right-angle corners. Then use the gingham as a pattern to cut around for the patterned fabric and the batting (wadding).

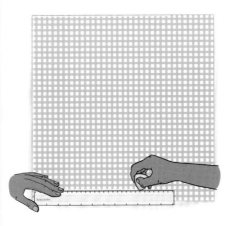

3 Lay the cotton batting on the table with the gingham fabric right side up on top of it. Place the patterned fabric on top of that, with the right side facing down. Pin all the way around all four sides through all the layers. Baste (tack) through all the layers, removing the pins as you sew.

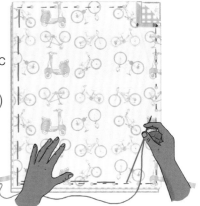

4 Make two marks with tailor's chalk about 5 in. (12 cm) apart along one long side. These will show you where to begin and end stitching so that you remember to leave a gap. Start at one chalk mark and machine stitch all the way around the fabric to the other mark, stitching ⅝ in. (1.5 cm) from the edge. Always remember to start and finish machine stitching securely (see page 114). Take out the basting stitches. Cut the corners off with scissors, making sure that you do not cut into the stitching; this will make the corners look neater.

Keep your laptop SAFE!

5 Turn the fabric right side out, through the gap. Push the corners out with the end of a pencil. Thread a needle and hand stitch the gap closed, pushing the seam allowance inside and using small, neat slipstitches (see page 113). Start and finish with a few small stitches to hold the thread securely.

6 Lay the fabric panel on the table with the patterned side up and a short side at the top. Lay the ribbon along the panel 4 in. (10 cm) from one long side and pin it in place. When you get to the top of the fabric, make a handle using 11 in. (28 cm) of ribbon, being careful not to twist it, and then pin it down the other long side, again 4 in. (10 cm) from the outer edge. Make another handle at the bottom, bring the ribbon back to where you started pinning, and overlap the ends. Baste the ribbon in place, then take out the pins.

7 Machine stitch along the outside edge of the ribbon on the left side of the panel. When you reach the top, with the needle through the fabric, turn the panel through a right angle and stitch along the base of the handle, then turn it again and stitch along the inner edge of the ribbon. Turn again at the other handle, stitching back to where you started. Do the same for the ribbon on the right-hand side. Take the basting stitches out.

8 Fold the panel in half to make the bag and pin down the sides. Baste in place, taking out the pins as you sew. Machine stitch down both sides, close to the edge. Take out the basting stitches.

9 To add a finishing touch, sew buttons onto the ribbon just below the handles (see page 117). This is just for decoration, so you can miss out this step if you like.

Sleepover bag

Keep all the essentials for a fun sleepover in this handy bag. Big enough to hold pajamas and clean clothes, there are also pockets for your comb, toothbrush, and even candy for a midnight feast!

You will need

One 12-in. (30-cm) square of gingham fabric for the pocket

Two 12 x 16-in. (30 x 40-cm) rectangles of patterned fabric for the bag (see page 112 for tips about cutting out rectangles of fabric)

32 in. (80 cm) cotton tape for the handles

Contrasting thread for basting (tacking)

Sewing threads to match the fabrics

Pins

Ruler

Tailor's chalk

Sewing needle

Scissors

Sewing machine

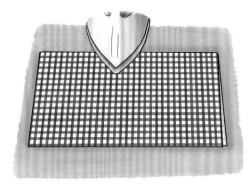

1 Fold the gingham fabric in half and ask an adult to help you press along the fold.

2 Place one of the patterned fabric rectangles right side up on the table. Lay the gingham pocket across the bottom; the fold of the gingham will form the top of the pocket. Pin around the three edges of the pocket to hold it in place (but not across the top folded edge). Baste (tack) around the pocket, taking the pins out as you go.

3 Measure along the top of the pocket and mark the center with tailor's chalk, then do the same along the bottom of the pocket. Draw a chalk line joining up the two marks, then sew a line of basting stitches along your chalked line. Use the lines of the gingham as a guide to help you stitch in a straight line.

4 Using thread to match the gingham fabric, machine stitch down the middle of the pocket, following the line of basting stitches. Remember always to begin and end the machine stitching securely (see page 114). Take out the basting stitches down the middle of the pocket, but leave them in place around the edge.

5 Lay the first rectangle on your table with the pocket facing up, then place the other fabric rectangle right side down on top of it, matching the edges carefully. Pin them together around three sides, leaving the top end (not the pocket end) open. Baste around the three sides, then take out the pins. Using thread to match the fabric, machine stitch the sides, then take out the basting stitches. Take out the basting stitches from around the pocket, too.

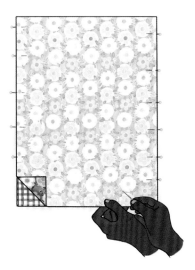

6 Turn the bag the right way out, pushing the corners out neatly with the blunt end of a pencil. Ask an adult to help you turn the top edge to the inside of the bag by ⅜ in. (1 cm) and to press it with an iron. Then ask the adult to turn it over again, by another 1½ in. (4 cm) and to press it again. Pin and baste it in place.

7 Machine stitch around the top of the bag, stitching about ¼ in. (5 mm) from the bottom folded edge.

8 Cut the cotton tape in half to make two handles. Fold the cut ends under by 1¼ in. (3 cm) and make a firm crease. Now pin one handle onto the outside of one side of the bag. Pin it so that the ends of the handle are 2 in. (5 cm) from the side seams, with the folded-up ends against the bag fabric so you can't see them. The bottom of the handle should be in line with the stitching around the top of the bag. Now pin the other handle onto the other side of the bag, exactly opposite the first one. Baste the handles in place and take out all the pins.

9 Machine stitch around the ends of the handles in a square shape. When you reach a corner, make sure that the needle is down in the fabric (if it is not, use the wheel at the side of the machine to lower it), raise the presser foot, turn the bag through a right angle, lower the presser foot, and stitch along the next side of the square. Keep doing this until you get back to where you started. This makes the handle really strong and secure. Take out the basting stitches and your bag is ready to use!

MP3 player case

Listen to your favorite music in style with this handy MP3 player case. The short ribbons can be tied to keep your MP3 player safe inside the bag, and the long ribbon makes a handy strap to put around your neck.

You will need

12 x 6 in. (30 x 15 cm) fabric

Contrasting thread for basting (tacking)

Sewing thread to match the fabric

56 in. (140 cm) narrow ribbon

Squared paper, ruler, and pencil

Pins

Pinking shears

Sewing needle

Sewing machine

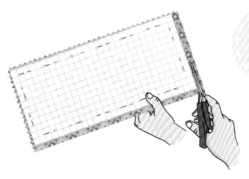

1 Measure and draw a rectangle 11 x 5 in. (28 x 12 cm) on squared paper and cut it out. Pin it onto the fabric, then cut around the edges with the pinking shears so that the fabric will not fray.

2 Turn the two short edges of the fabric over to the wrong side by ⅝ in. (1.5 cm) and pin them in place. Baste (tack) along both ends, removing the pins as you go. Thread your machine with thread to match the fabric, then machine stitch along the short ends. Take the basting stitches out.

3 Cut two pieces of ribbon 8 in. (20 cm) long. Pin one ribbon to the middle of each short end of the fabric, on the wrong side, overlapping the ribbon onto the fabric by 1 in. (2.5 cm). Baste the ribbons in place, then take out the pins. Machine stitch the ribbons, using the reverse on the machine to stitch backward and forward a few times to secure the ribbons. Take out the basting stitches.

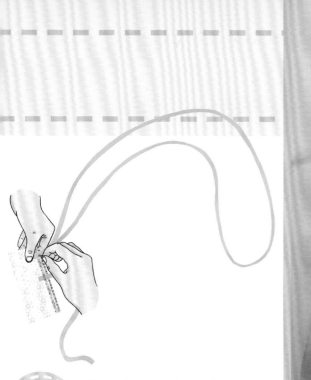

4 Take the remaining ribbon and fold it in half to make a loop. Pin the raw ends beside one of the other ribbons ¾ in. (2 cm) away from one long edge, again overlapping the ribbon onto the fabric by 1 in. (2.5 cm). Baste and machine stitch in place in the same way as you did the other two ribbons. Take out the basting stitches.

TIP
For tips on how to sew on a ribbon without basting first, see page 116.

5 Fold the fabric in half with right sides together and pin the sides together. Baste the sides, removing the pins as you stitch. Be very careful not to get the ribbons caught in the seams. Machine stitch along both sides, remembering to begin and end your stitching securely (see page 114). Take out the basting stitches and turn the bag the right way out.

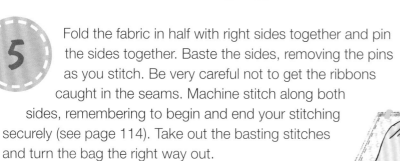

Chapter 3

Things for Your Room

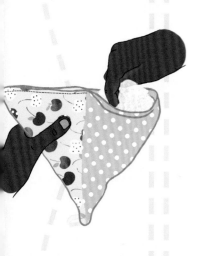

Flower chain

This chain of brightly colored felt shapes will brighten up any dull corner of your room. Use scraps of felt, if you have them, or visit a craft store where you can often buy packs of different-colored felts. You don't have to use the templates; you could make your own designs—diamonds, leaves, butterflies—use your imagination!

You will need

Templates on page 121

3-in. (8-cm) square of felt for each flower shape or circle

White sewing thread

Contrasting thread for basting (tacking)

24 in. (60 cm) ribbon, ⅜ in. (1 cm) wide

Paper for pattern

Pencil

Scissors

Pins

Sewing machine

Sewing needle

1 Trace the templates on page 121 onto paper and cut out a flower shape or circle. Pin the paper template to the felt and cut it out neatly. Cut out 26 more flowers or circles in the same way—this will make a chain that is about 60 in. (150 cm) long.

2 Arrange the felt shapes on the table, making sure that each shape is next to one in a different color. Pile the shapes up in the order that you have arranged them in.

3 Thread your sewing machine with white thread. Take the top felt shape from your pile and machine stitch across the center, remembering to start the machine stitching securely (see page 114). Try to keep your stitching straight, but don't worry too much about it—the chain will look great even if your stitches are a little bit wobbly! Make a few machine stitches after the felt shape, then take the next felt shape from your pile and stitch across this shape in the same way. Continue until you have stitched all the shapes together in a long chain.

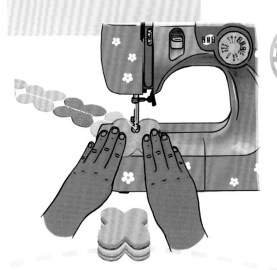

4 Cut the ribbon into two pieces that are 12 in. (30 cm) long. Fold one piece in half to find the center and pin it to the felt shape at one end of the chain about ⅜ in. (1 cm) from the edge. Baste (tack) it in place, remove the pin, and then machine stitch, using the reverse on the machine to stitch backward and forward a few times. (For tips on how to sew on a ribbon without basting first, see page 116.) Do the same with the other piece of ribbon at the other end of the chain. Use the ribbons to hang the chain up.

Patchwork pillow

This will really brighten up your room and is quick and easy to make, with only seven straight seams. Patchwork is a great way to use up scraps of material. You can even cut up favorite worn-out clothes (ask first!) or you can go out and choose some really funky fabrics.

You will need

Four different fabrics, each at least 28¾ x 5⅛ in. (73 x 13 cm)

Contrasting thread for basting (tacking)

Sewing threads to match the fabrics

12 x 16-in. (30 x 40-cm) pillow form (cushion pad)

Pins

Sewing needle

Tape measure

Sewing machine

Notes: You should sew all the seams ⅝ in. (1.5 cm) from the edge.

Pressing
You need to press the fabric lots of times with a hot iron in this project; always ask an adult to help you to do this.

1 If your fabric needs to be cut to size, use a piece of newspaper or brown wrapping paper to cut out a 28¾ x 5⅛-in. (73 x 13-cm) rectangle of paper. (See page 112 for tips on cutting rectangles.) Use this as a pattern: pin it to each of the fabrics in turn and cut out the four rectangles.

2 Decide what order you want the fabrics to go in and lay them out on your table. Place the second strip on top of the first, with right sides together, and pin and baste (tack) them together along the right-hand edge. Take out the pins. Machine stitch the strips together, then take out the basting stitches. Always remember to start and finish machine stitching securely (see page 114). Ask an adult to help you press the seam open with an iron. Join the third and fourth strips together in the same way.

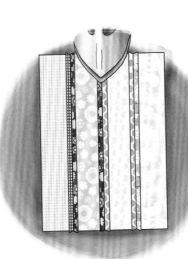

3 With right sides together, place the second pair of strips on top of the first. Pin and baste them together along the right-hand edge, as before. Take out the pins, then machine stitch. Turn the piece over and press the seam open with an iron. Turn the piece over and press it again on the right side.

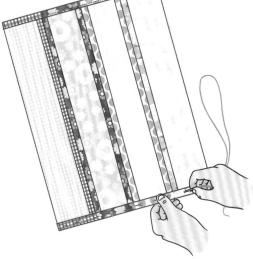

4 Place the fabric on the table, with the right side facing down. Turn the top and bottom edges over by ⅝ in. (1.5 cm). Pin and baste, then take out the pins. Machine stitch across the top and bottom edges, stitching ⅜ in. (1 cm) from the folded edge. Take out the basting stitches. Press.

5 Place the fabric on the table, with the right side up facing up. Fold the top down by 8 in. (20 cm); measure this with your tape measure. Pin the edges to hold it in place.

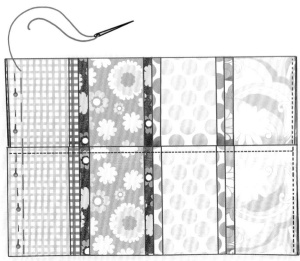

 6 Now fold the bottom edge up by 8 in. (20 cm), again measuring it with a tape measure. It will overlap the top fold. Pin and baste the two side edges right along the side of the cushion, then take out the pins. Machine stitch along both sides, then take out the basting stitches.

Colorful and COMFY!

7 Turn the cover right side out and press. Push the pillow form (cushion pad) inside the cover, pull the corners into place, and smooth out the cover.

Pencil roll

A special set of pens or pencils deserves to be kept together and kept safe. This handy pencil roll is perfect for that. It is very easy to make and is practical as well as looking great—the flap across the top means that nothing can fall out, and the whole thing can be rolled up tightly to put in your bag.

You will need

20 x 16 in. (50 x 40 cm) patterned fabric

18 x 24 in. (45 x 60 cm) gingham fabric

28 in. (70 cm) ribbon, ⅝ in. (1.5 cm) wide

Contrasting thread for basting (tacking)

Sewing thread to match the fabric

Newspaper or brown wrapping paper for pattern

Pins

Scissors

Ruler

Tailor's chalk or non-permanent fabric marker pen

Sewing needle

Sewing machine

1 Use a piece of newspaper or brown wrapping paper to cut out a 17½ x 12½-in. (44 x 32-cm) rectangle of paper. (See page 112 for tips on cutting rectangles.) Pin it to the patterned fabric and cut it out. Now mark a 16 x 22½-in. (40 x 57-cm) rectangle directly onto the gingham and cut it out—the squares will help you draw true right angles and cut straight lines.

2 Lay the patterned fabric on the table, with the wrong side facing up. Place the gingham fabric on top of it right side up, about ¾ in. (2 cm) from the top edge and the sides. Put a few pins along the top edge to hold the gingham in place.

¾ in. (2 cm)

¾ in. (2 cm)

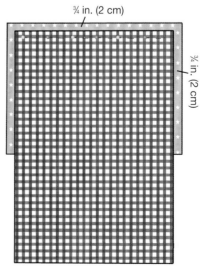

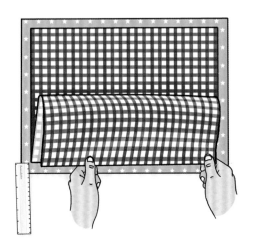

3 Using your ruler to check you've got the distance right, fold the bottom edge of the gingham fabric up so that the fold is ¾ in. (2 cm) above the bottom edge of the patterned fabric. Crease it well. Now fold the top edge of the gingham back down so that the edge meets the bottom folded edge. This will make the pocket. Pin and baste (tack) all the way around the gingham fabric to hold it in place.

4 Using your ruler and tailor's chalk or a non-permanent fabric pen, make marks 1½ in. (4 cm) apart along the top and bottom of the gingham (counting squares on the gingham might make this easier), then draw long lines to join up the marks. Thread your sewing machine with thread to match the fabric and stitch along these lines. Always remember to start and finish machine stitching securely (see page 114).

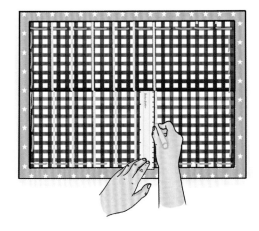

5 Take out all the basting stitches. Fold the patterned fabric over by ⅜ in. (1 cm) along all four sides and ask an adult to help you press it with an iron to keep it in place.

6 Fold the patterned fabric over by another ⅜ in. (1 cm) and pin and baste it in place. Take out the pins, then stitch all the way around with the machine, sewing as close to the inside edge of the patterned fabric as you can.

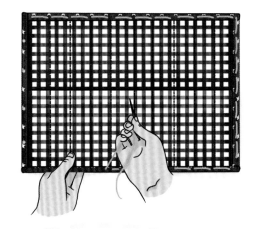

7 Turn the pencil roll so that the outside patterned fabric is facing up. Fold the ribbon in half to find the center. Pin the center of the ribbon onto the patterned fabric 4 in. (10 cm) from the bottom edge and ⅜ in. (1 cm) from the right-hand side edge. Baste, remove the pin, and machine stitch across the ribbon, using the reverse on the machine to stitch backward and forward a few times to secure it. (For a tip about how to set on ribbon without basting first, see page 116.) Fill the pockets on the inside of the roll with pens and pencils, and then fold the top flap over. Roll the fabric up and tie with the ribbon to hold it all neatly together.

Wall tidy

Use this pretty hanging wall tidy to store your trinkets and treasures. If you only have one hook on the back of the door, you could hang the wall tidy on a coat hanger first. It is a good idea to use quite thick fabric, especially for the backing, then the tidy will hold its shape and not sag when the pockets are full (but not too thick or it will be difficult to sew).

You will need

16 x 30 in. (40 x 75 cm) patterned fabric

16 x 20 in. (40 x 50 cm) heavyweight fabric for the backing

20 in. (50 cm) cotton tape or ribbon, ½ in. (12 mm) wide

Contrasting thread for basting (tacking)

Sewing thread to match the fabric

Newspaper or brown wrapping paper for pattern

Pencil and ruler

Pins

Sewing needle

Tape measure

Sewing machine

Scissors

Blunt pencil

Tailor's chalk

1 Draw a 14-in. (36-cm) square and a 14 x 18½-in. (36 x 47-cm) rectangle on newspaper or brown wrapping paper and cut them out. (See page 112 for tips on cutting squares and rectangles.) Fold the patterned fabric so that it is doubled, pin on the square paper pattern, and cut out two squares. Do the same with the paper rectangle on the heavy fabric; if you find it difficult to cut two pieces of the thick fabric at once, cut the rectangles out one at a time.

2 Fold one piece of patterned fabric in half, with right sides together. Pin and baste (tack) the long raw edges together. Take out the pins. Machine stitch, sewing ⅝ in. (1.5 cm) from the edge. Always remember to start and finish stitching securely (see page 114). Take out the basting stitches. Turn the fabric the right way out. Ask an adult to help you press the fabric with an iron so that the seam runs along the bottom edge. Do the same with the second piece of patterned fabric. These will be the pockets.

A PERFECT place to put things!

3 Cut the ribbon in half so that you have two pieces that are 10 in. (25 cm) long. Place one piece of backing fabric right side up on the table. Fold a piece of ribbon in half to make a loop. Pin and baste the cut ends of one ribbon to the top edge of the fabric, 4 in. (10 cm) from the corner. (For tips on how to sew on a ribbon without basting first, see page 116.) Do the same with the second piece of ribbon, 4 in. (10 cm) from the other corner. Take out the pins.

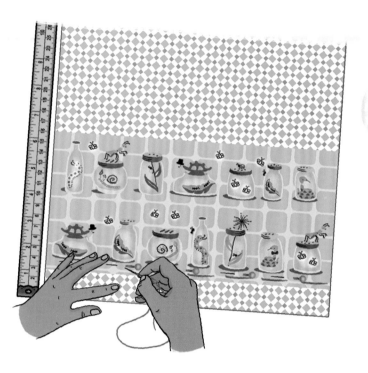

4 Place the other piece of backing fabric right side up on the table. Place a pocket, with the seam at the bottom, 1 in. (2.5 cm) from the bottom edge; use your tape measure to check it's the same distance from the bottom edge all the way along. Pin and baste the pocket to the backing fabric along the bottom edge, then take out the pins. Machine stitch the pocket in place along the bottom edge, sewing close to the pocket edge.

5 Pin the other pocket (again with the seam at the bottom) onto the backing fabric ¾ in. (2 cm) above the top edge of the first pocket and pin, baste, and machine stitch along the bottom edge, as before. Take out all the basting stitches.

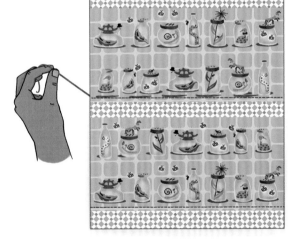

6 Place the backing piece with the ribbons right side up on the table (with ribbons at the top), then put the backing piece with the pockets right side down on top of it (with openings to the top), matching up the edges. Pin and baste all the way around, then take out the pins. Make two marks with tailor's chalk about 5 in. (12 cm) apart along the bottom edge. These will show you where to begin and end stitching so that you remember to leave a gap.

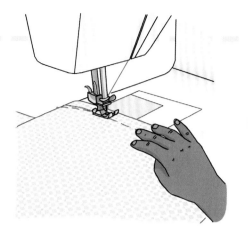

7 Starting at one chalk mark, machine stitch all the way around the tidy to the other mark, sewing ⅝ in (1.5 cm) from the edge. Take out the basting stitches.

8 Snip off the corners, making sure that you do not cut through the stitching. Turn the wall tidy the right way out, then push the corners out neatly using the blunt end of a pencil.

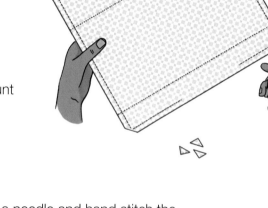

9 Thread a needle and hand stitch the gap closed, using small, neat slipstitches (see page 113).

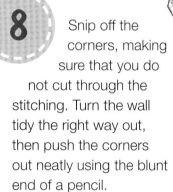

10 Turn the wall tidy over so that you're looking at the back. Measure the width of the wall tidy at the top and then find the halfway point and mark it with tailor's chalk. Do the same in the middle and on the bottom edge. Join up your points with a ruler. Machine stitch along this line to make four pockets.

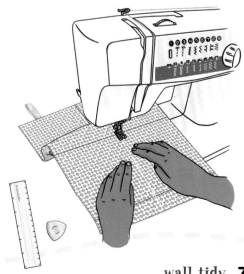

Stripy quilt

Once you have learnt to keep the machine going straight, it doesn't take much more time to sew a long seam than a short one, so this quirky quilt isn't that hard. However, there is a lot of fabric to work with, so it is best to have your sewing machine on a big table. Choose a bright, bold pattern for the wider band of fabric so that it will really stand out and use machine-washable batting (wadding).

You will need

Four different fabrics, each measuring 11 x 44 in. (28 x 110 cm)

17 x 44 in. (43 x 110 cm) patterned fabric

56 x 44 in. (143 x 110 cm) spotty fabric for the backing

56 x 44 in. (143 x 110 cm) cotton batting (wadding)

Contrasting thread for basting (tacking)

Sewing thread to match the fabric

Tape measure

Pins

Sewing needle

Scissors

Sewing machine

Tailor's chalk

Blunt pencil

1 To get rectangles of the large pieces of fabric you need for this project, it is easiest to rip it! Fabric will rip in straight lines. Make sure that the end of the fabric is straight, then measure the length you need (for example, 11 in./28 cm for the stripes), make a small nick in the side with a pair of scissors, and rip it apart.

2 Arrange the fabric pieces for the stripes on the floor in the order you want.

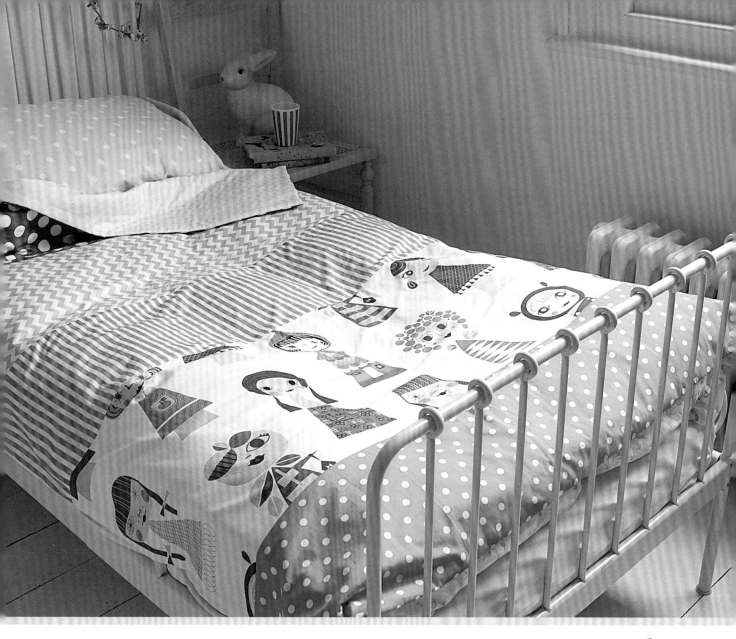

A quirky QUILT for your bed

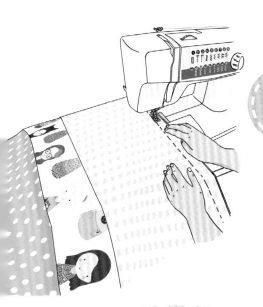

3 With right sides together, pin and then baste (tack) the top two pieces of fabric together along one long edge. Take out the pins. Machine stitch the pieces of fabric together, stitching ⅝ in. (1.5 cm) from the edge. (Remember to start and finish machine stitching securely—see page 114.) Take out the basting stitches. Join on the remaining pieces of fabric in the same way, taking out the basting stitches after you have machined each seam. Ask an adult to help you press the patchwork panel, pressing the seams open on the back of it.

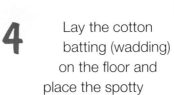

4 Lay the cotton batting (wadding) on the floor and place the spotty backing fabric right side up on top of it. Place the patchwork panel on top, with the right side facing down, making sure that all the edges line up. Pin all the way around, then baste, taking out the pins as you go. Make two marks with tailor's chalk about 10 in. (25 cm) apart on the bottom edge. These will show you where to begin and end stitching so that you remember to leave a gap.

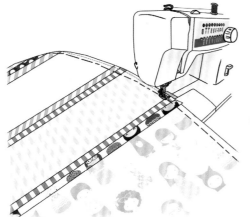

 Starting at one chalk mark, machine stitch all the way around to the other mark, sewing ⅝ in. (1.5 cm) from the edge. Take out the basting stitches.

6 Snip off the corners, making sure that you do not cut through the stitching. Turn the quilt right side out by pushing the fabric through the gap. Push the corners out with a blunt pencil.

 Thread a needle and hand stitch the gap closed, using small neat slipstitches.

Appliquéd pillowcase ☺ ☺ ☺

To make this bold, bright pillowcase you need to use fusible bonding web—this is a magic material that allows you to stick one fabric to another. Once you have used it for this project, you will see the endless possibilities for making your own appliqué designs.

You will need

Templates on page 123

14-in. (35-cm) square of fusible bonding web

Red fabric, approx. 12 in. (30 cm) square

Approx 8 x 4 in. (20 x 10 cm) green fabric

Approx. 5 x 2 in. (12 x 5 cm) brown fabric

(These colored pieces do not need to be exact rectangles—just big enough to fit the templates on)

Two 22 x 16-in. (56 x 40-cm) rectangles of gingham fabric (see page 112 for tips about cutting out squares and rectangles of fabric)

47 in. (120 cm) ribbon, ¼ in. (7 mm) wide

White thread for sewing

Contrasting thread for basting (tacking)

20 x 14-in. (50 x 35-cm) pillow

Tracing paper, scrap paper, and pencil (optional)

Pins

Scissors

Sewing needle

Sewing machine

1 Photocopy the templates on page 123 or trace them onto a scrap paper. Cut three pieces of fusible bonding web big enough to roughly fit each of the apple, leaf, and stalk templates. Put the pieces of fusible bonding web rough side down on the wrong side of the red (apple), green (leaf), and brown (stalk) fabrics and ask an adult to help you press them with an iron, so that they stick to the fabric.

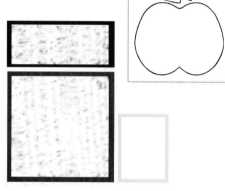

2 Now cut out the apple template carefully and put it on the fusible bonding web side of the red fabric. Draw around it and cut out. In the same way, cut out the leaf from the green fabric and the stalk from the brown fabric.

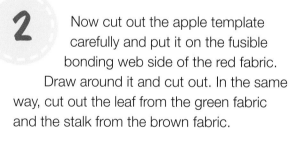

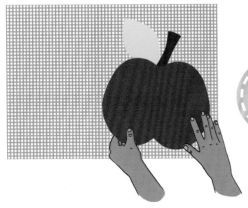

3 Peel the backing papers off the apple, leaf, and stalk and arrange them on the bottom right-hand corner of one of the pieces of gingham fabric—not too close to the edge. Lay a clean dish towel over the top and ask an adult to help you press the shapes with an iron, which will stick them to the gingham. Let the fabrics cool before you pick them up.

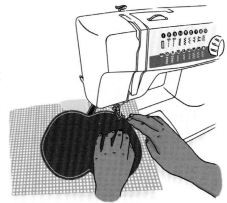

4 The fusible bonding web will hold the fabrics in place, but stitching it gives it added strength, especially if you want to wash the pillowcase. However, if this step is a bit too fiddly for you then you can miss it out. Machine stitch around the shapes, stitching about ¼ in. (5 mm) from the edges of the fabrics and sewing slowly to help you keep to the shapes.

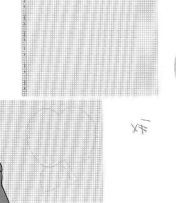

5 Take the two gingham fabric pieces and turn under ⅝ in. (1.5 cm) to the wrong side along one short end (the opposite end to the apple decoration on the decorated piece). Baste (tack) along the edge of both pieces of fabric and remove the pins as you go. Machine stitch in place. Always remember to start and finish machine stitching securely (see page 114). Take out the basting stitches.

6 Fold the ribbon in half and cut it, then fold each piece in half again and cut them so that you have four equal pieces. Pin two ribbons on the wrong side of the hemmed edge of each piece of gingham. Pin one 4 in. (10 cm) from the top, the other 4 in. (10 cm) from the bottom. Baste in place, then take out the pins. Machine stitch across the ribbons, using the reverse on the machine to stitch backward and forward a few times to hold the ribbons securely in place.

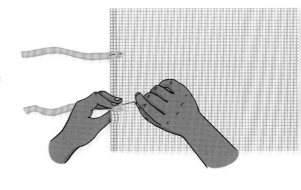

TIP

For tips on how to sew on a ribbon without basting first, see page 116.

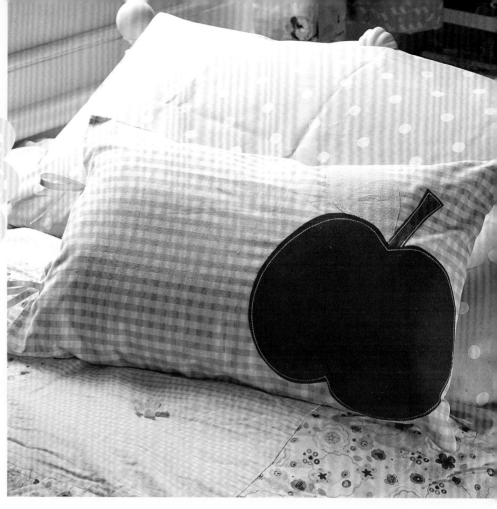

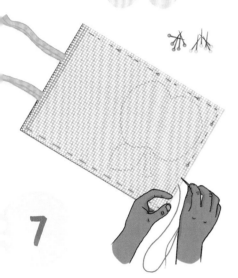

Appliqué an APPLE

7

With right sides together, pin the gingham pieces together, making sure that the ends with the ribbons match up. Baste around three sides (leaving the ribboned end open), removing the pins as you go. Machine stitch around the three sides, sewing ⅝ in. (1.5 cm) from the edge. Take out the basting stitches.

8 Snip the corners off diagonally, making sure that you do not cut into the stitching. Turn the pillowcase the right way out and push the corners out neatly.

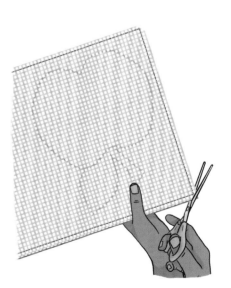

9 Ask an adult to help you press the pillowcase with an iron and then put the pillow in the case and tie the ribbons in to neat bows.

Ribbon pillow

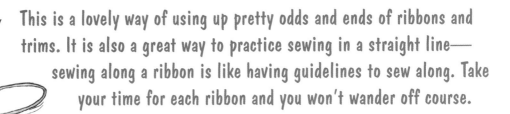

This is a lovely way of using up pretty odds and ends of ribbons and trims. It is also a great way to practice sewing in a straight line—sewing along a ribbon is like having guidelines to sew along. Take your time for each ribbon and you won't wander off course.

You will need

Two 12 x 9-in. (30 x 22-cm) pieces of fabric (see page 112 for tips about cutting out squares and rectangles of fabric)

Selection of ribbons and rick-rack braids in 9-in. (22-cm) lengths

White thread

Polyester toy filling

Pins

Sewing needle

Tailor's chalk

Sewing machine

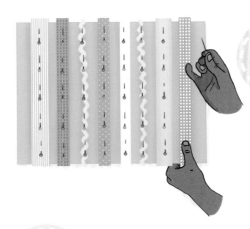

1 Place one piece of fabric right side up on the table. Spread the ribbons and rick-rack braid out across the fabric, moving them around until they look just right. Pin them in place.

2 Baste (tack) the ribbons and rick-rack in place, removing the pins as you go. Machine stitch along the middle of each ribbon. Try using the zig-zag stitch on your machine to sew some of the ribbons—it will look pretty. Take out the basting stitches. Trim the ends of the ribbons and braids so that they're level with the edges of the fabric.

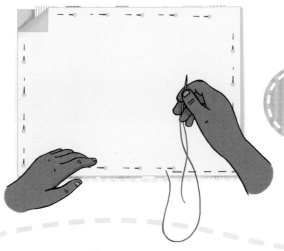

3 Take the second piece of fabric and lay it on top of the first, with the right sides together, lining up the edges. Pin, then baste all the way around the edges, taking the pins out as you stitch.

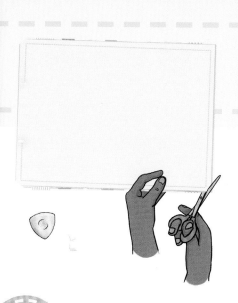

4 Make two marks with tailor's chalk about 3 in. (8 cm) apart along one short side. These will show you where to begin and end stitching so that you remember to leave a gap for turning and stuffing the pillow. Start at one mark and machine stitch around the fabric to the other mark, stitching ⅝ in. (1.5 cm) from the edge. Remember to start and finish machine stitching securely (see page 114). Take out the basting stitches. Cut the corners off with scissors, making sure that you do not cut into the stitching. This will make the corners look neater when you turn the cover right side out.

Use up your scraps of RIBBON

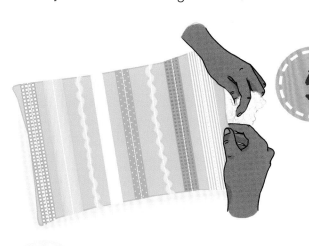

5 Turn the cover right side out and push the corners out with the blunt end of a pencil. Ask an adult to help you press the cover to remove any creases. Fill the cover with toy filling.

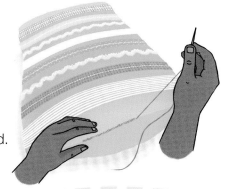

6 Thread a needle, then turn the seam allowance inside at the opening and slipstitch (see page 113) the opening closed. Start and finish with a few small stitches to secure the thread.

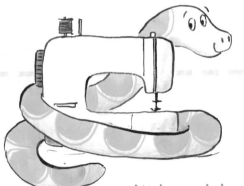

Pencil pots

These pretty pencil pots will tidy up your desk at home, but are also great to give as gifts to friends and relatives—everyone needs a pencil pot beside their phone or in their kitchen and these look much more stylish than the old mugs most people use!

You will need

14 x 9½ in. (36 x 24 cm) thick canvas

14 x 9½ in. (36 x 24 cm) patterned fabric

Sewing thread to match the fabric

Contrasting thread for basting (tacking)

Pins

Sewing needle

Sewing machine

1 Lay the patterned fabric right side down on the canvas fabric and pin them together along one long side. Baste (tack), removing the pins as you go. Machine stitch in place, then take out the basting stitches. Always remember to start and finish machine stitching securely (see page 114).

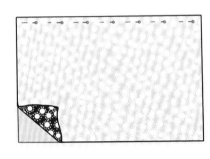

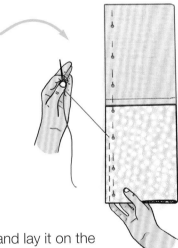

2 Open out the fabric and lay it on the table so that the patterned fabric is at the bottom with the right side facing up. Take the right side of the fabric and fold it in half over to the left. Pin down the long side to make a tube. Baste, then take out the pins. Machine stitch along the side and take out the basting stitches.

TIP

See page 112 for tips about cutting out rectangles of fabric.

PRETTY POTS for pencils and pens

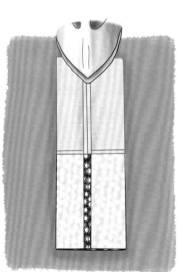

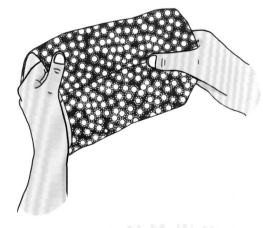

3 With the help of an adult, press the long seam open, then turn the tube right side out and press the right side as well.

4 Push the canvas part of the tube down inside the patterned part, making sure that the seam that joined the two fabrics runs around the top of the tube.

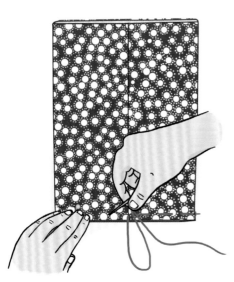

5 Lay the tube on the table, with the seam in the middle facing up, and flatten the tube. Pin along the bottom raw edge and baste. Machine stitch along the edge and take out the basting stitches.

6 Lay the tube down again, this time with the seam at the side, and flatten the base of the tube the other way, so that the bottom seam you have just sewn is folded in half. This will make two points on top of each other at the base of the tube. Pin across one point 1¾ in. (4.5 cm) from the tip. Baste along this line, removing the pins as you go, and then machine stitch. Remove the basting stitches. Do the same for the other point.

7 Turn the tube canvas side out and then fold the top over to form the rim. Push the flaps down inside the base.

Pyramid doorstop

This colorful doorstop is just the thing for keeping your door ajar. Choose bright, co-ordinating fabrics and add a handy ribbon loop, so that it can be hung on the door handle when it is not needed. Filling the doorstop with dried lentils or peas will make it nice and heavy.

You will need

8 in. (20 cm) ribbon, ⅜ in. (1 cm) wide

Two 9-in. (23-cm) squares of fabric (see page 112 for tips about cutting out squares and rectangles of fabric)

Sewing thread to match the fabric

Contrasting thread for basting (tacking)

Polyester toy filling

1lb (500 g) dried lentils or peas

Pins

Sewing needle

Sewing machine

1 Fold the ribbon in half to make a loop and pin it to the right side of one corner of a fabric square, with the looped end facing diagonally inward and the raw ends of the ribbon sticking out by 1 in. (2.5 cm). Baste (tack) it in place, then take out the pin. Machine stitch across the ribbon, using the reverse on the machine to stitch backward and forward a few times to hold the ribbon firmly in place. (For tips on how to sew on a ribbon without basting first, see page 116.) You can miss out this step if you don't want a ribbon handle on your doorstop.

2 With right sides together, lay the fabric squares on top of each other. Pin around three sides of the squares, leaving one side open. Baste (tack) around the three pinned sides, taking out the pins as you stitch.

3 Machine stitch around the three basted sides, sewing ⅝ in. (1.5 cm) from the edge. Always remember to start and finish machine stitching securely (see page 114)—especially for this project, as any loose stitching could lead to leaking lentils! Take out the basting stitches. Turn the bag shape the right way out.

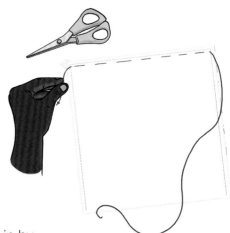

4 Turn the edges of the open side in by ⅝ in. (1.5 cm) and ask an adult to help you press them with an iron.

5 Open the bag and then push the side seams at the top together so that the bag will have a pyramid shape. Pin along half of the top edge, baste, remove the pins, and then machine stitch halfway across the side, keeping close to the edge.

6 Push a few handfuls of polyester toy filling inside the bag (through the gap left across the top) so that the bag is about half full.

7 Use a funnel (or make one from a piece of rolled-up paper) and pour in the dried lentils or peas until the bag is nearly full.

Keep your DOOR ajar

8 Squeeze the stuffing and lentils up to the top of the bag and pin and baste with small stitches across the opening about 1 in. (2.5 cm) from the edge. This will keep the lentils or peas well away from the machine when you are stitching! Remove the pins and machine stitch close to the edge, overlapping the stitching on the other half to make sure that there are no gaps for the lentils to escape from.

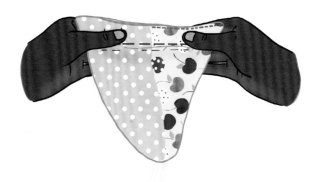

Needle case

Every sewing kit needs a needle case and with this stylish fabric one you will never lose your needles again. Stitch one for yourself using a favorite fabric or make one as a gift for a friend—it will be used and treasured for many years to come.

You will need

Two 8½ x 6-in. (21 x 15-cm) pieces of fabric (see page 112 for tips about cutting out squares and rectangles of fabric)

Two 7 x 4½-in. (17 x 11-cm) pieces of felt

6 in. (15 cm) thin ribbon

One button, ¾ in. (2 cm) in diameter

Contrasting thread for basting (tacking)

Thread to match the fabric

Pins

Sewing needle

Pinking shears

Sewing machine

Ruler

Tailor's chalk

Safety pin (optional)

1 Place the pieces of fabric wrong sides together, matching up the edges. Pin them together and baste (tack) around the edge, removing the pins as you go. Thread your machine with thread to match the fabric, and machine stitch around all four sides, sewing ⅝ in. (1.5 cm) from the edges. Always remember to start and finish machine stitching securely (see page 114). Take out the basting stitches.

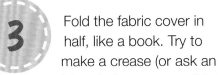

2 Using the pinking shears, cut around the edges of the fabric, making sure that you do not cut into the stitches.

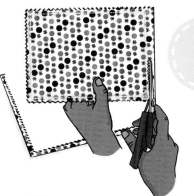
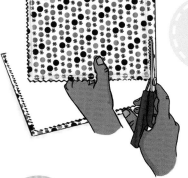

3 Fold the fabric cover in half, like a book. Try to make a crease (or ask an adult to help you press it in half with an iron) and mark the top and bottom of the crease with some tailor's chalk. Now put the two pieces of felt on top of each other, pin them together, and fold them in half to find the center. Crease them and mark the top and bottom of the crease with chalk. Use a ruler and chalk to join up the chalk marks, so that you have a line down the center. Pin the center of the felt to the center of the fabric to make a book, lining up the chalk marks. Make sure that the pins go through all the layers.

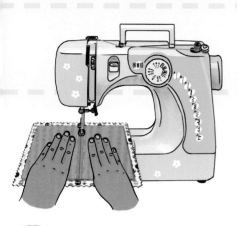

4 Making sure that you stitch through all layers, baste the felt and fabric together. Take out the pins. Machine stitch along the chalk line and then take out the basting stitches.

TIP

For tips on how to sew on a ribbon without basting first, see page 116.

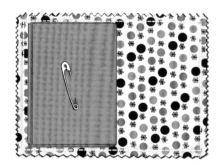

5 Open the needle case, and pin all the pages to the inside of the front cover with a safety pin to hold them out of the way. Turn the needle case over.

6 Fold the ribbon into a loop and pin it onto the outside of the back cover, making sure that it is the same distance from the top and the bottom. The ends of the ribbon should overlap the edge of the case by 1¼ in. (3 cm). Baste it in place, remove the pin, and then machine stitch about ⅝ in. (1.5 cm) from the edge, using the reverse on the machine to stitch backward and forward a few times, which will secure the ribbon. Take out the basting stitches and the safety pin that's holding the felt pages in place.

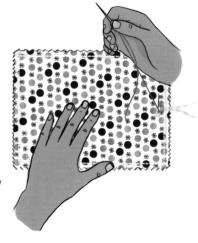

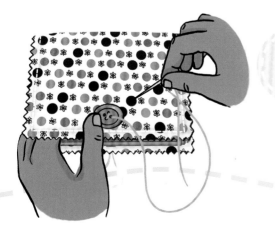

7 Close the needle case. Fold the loop of ribbon onto the front of the cover and make a mark at the end of the loop to show you where the button needs to go. Sew the button in place (see page 117) and loop the ribbon over the button to close the case.

Lavender bag

Everyone loves a lavender bag! It's the perfect thing to put in your wardrobe to keep your clothes smelling lovely and fresh. These simple little bags are very easy to make and take no time at all, so you could stitch lots of them to give as gifts—or why not sell them at a fair to raise money for charity?

You will need

6¼ x 9½ in. (16 x 24 cm) fabric (see page 112 for tips about cutting out squares and rectangles of fabric)

12 in. (30 cm) narrow ribbon

Contrasting thread for basting (tacking)

Thread to match the fabric

About two handfuls of dried lavender

Scissors

Pins

Sewing needle

Sewing machine

Pinking shears

Teaspoon

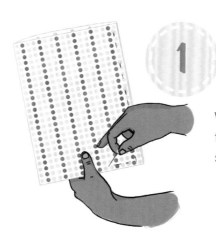

1 Fold the fabric in half lengthwise and then cut along the fold, so that you have two pieces measuring 6¼ x 4¾ in. (16 x 12 cm). With wrong sides together, pin them together on three sides, leaving one short edge open.

2 Baste (tack) around the three pinned sides, taking out the pins as you go. Machine stitch around the three sides, stitching ⅝ in. (1.5 cm) from the outside edge—but start and finish your stitching ⅝ in. (1.5 cm) from the top edge on each side. Always remember to start and finish machine stitching securely (see page 114).

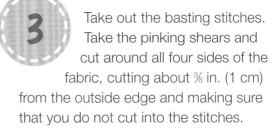

3 Take out the basting stitches. Take the pinking shears and cut around all four sides of the fabric, cutting about ⅜ in. (1 cm) from the outside edge and making sure that you do not cut into the stitches.

4 Open the top of the bag and spoon the lavender inside.

5 Wrap the ribbon tightly around the top of the bag, knot it, and finish with a neat bow. You may need someone to help you with this bit—it is difficult to tie a tight knot on your own. Trim the ends of the ribbon so that they are both about the same length.

Chapter 4
Toys and Games

Rag doll

This lovable rag doll is made quite simply from two pieces of fabric stitched together. Choose her skin color, hair color, and the expression on her face. And when you have finished making her, turn to page 95 to find out how to make her lovely outfit.

You will need

Templates on pages 124–125

27½ x 24 in. (70 x 60 cm) muslin (calico)

20 x 6½ in. (50 x 16 cm) brown felt

Scrap of dark brown or black felt for eyes

Scrap of red felt for mouth

Sewing threads to match the muslin (calico) and felt

Contrasting thread for basting (tacking)

Polyester toy filling

20 in. (50 cm) ribbon, 1½ in. (4 cm) wide

Paper for patterns

Pencil

Scissors

Pins

Sewing needle

Sewing machine

1 Ask an adult to photocopy the doll body template on page 124 using the 200% zoom on the photocopier, and cut it out. Fold the muslin (calico) in half and place the template on it. Pin it in place and cut it out carefully, so that you have two doll shapes.

2 Trace the hair templates on page 125 and cut them out. Pin them onto brown felt and cut out one front hair piece and one back hair piece.

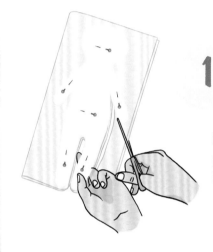

3 Thread your sewing machine with thread to match the felt. Pin the back hair piece to one of the doll shapes and machine stitch along the bottom edge. Always remember to start and finish machine stitching securely (see page 114). Pin the front hair piece to the other doll shape and machine stitch around the fringe, stitching close to the edge of the felt. Take out the pins.

What will you call your DOLL?

4 Trace the circle eye and heart mouth templates on page 124 and cut them out. Pin the circle shape to dark brown or black felt and cut out two felt circles for the eyes. Pin the heart shape to red felt and cut out one heart for the mouth. Thread a needle with thread to match the felt. Hand stitch the eyes and mouth onto the face, using a few small stitches on each.

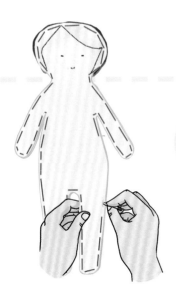

5 With right sides together (the sides with the felt hair stitched on), pin the two doll shapes together. Baste (tack) all the way around the doll, leaving a gap of about 4 in. (10 cm) in one side of the body, then take out the pins. Starting at one side of the gap, machine stitch around the doll, ⅝ in. (1.5 cm) from the edge, to the other side of the gap. Make sure you sew through the hair, too, when you sew around the top of the head. Take out the basting stitches and, using the tips of small sharp scissors, cut small snips into the seam allowance around all the curves, especially between the legs, under the arms, and around the head. Take care not to cut into the stitching.

6 Turn the doll right side out by carefully pushing the arms, legs, and head through the opening. Use the flat end of a pencil to push the ends of the arms and legs out. Ask an adult to help you press the doll on both sides with an iron. Take small pieces of toy filling and push them into the doll, again using the flat end of a pencil to push the filling down the arms and legs.

7 When you've finished stuffing the doll, fold the fabric in along the edges of the gap and slipstitch (see page 113) the gap closed.

8 Tie the ribbon in a neat bow and hand stitch it onto the doll's head, using small stitches so that they cannot be seen. Trim the ends of the ribbon to make them nice and tidy.

Doll's dress and shoes

This outfit is so easy to make that you'll be able to make several pretty dresses for your doll with matching shoes in no time. The dress is simply two squares of fabric sewn together with ribbon ties at the shoulders. The cute felt shoes are decorated with little buttons, but you could try bows or beads instead. This dress is perfect for the rag doll on page 92, but you could easily change the measurements and make it for other dolls and teddies, too.

You will need

12 x 24 in. (30 x 60 cm) of fabric for the dress

6-in. (15-cm) square of felt for the shoes

27½ in. (70 cm) ribbon, ¼ in. (7 mm) wide

Two small buttons to decorate the shoes

Contrasting thread for basting (tacking)

Sewing threads to match your fabric and the felt

Template on page 125

Squared paper

Pins

Tape measure

Scissors

Sewing needle

Sewing machine

Safety pin

Tracing paper and paper for pattern

Pencil

1 Use squared paper to cut out a 10½-in. (27-cm) square of paper. (See page 112 for tips on cutting squares and rectangles.) Fold the fabric in half, pin the paper square to the fabric, and cut it out to give you two fabric squares.

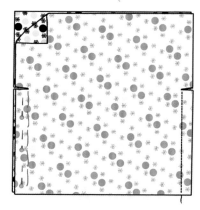

2 Lay one piece of fabric on top of the other, with right sides together. Pin them together along the sides. Measure 5 in. (12 cm) down the sides from the top corners and make a small snip ⅝ in. (1.5 cm) long on each side. Baste (tack) from the snip down to the bottom edge on both sides, take out the pins, then machine stitch, stitching ⅝ in. (1.5 cm) from the edge. Always remember to start and finish machine stitching securely (see page 114). Take out the basting stitches.

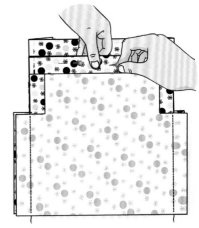

3 To finish the armholes neatly, fold the top layer of fabric above the snip over to the wrong side by ⅝ in. (1.5 cm) on each side of the dress, then do the same with the bottom layer. Pin and baste down each of these four flaps, then take out the pins. Machine stitch ⅜ in. (1 cm) from the folded edge. Take out the basting stitches.

4 Fold the top edge over by ¾ in. (2 cm) on the top layer of fabric, pin, and baste. Take out the pins. Machine stitch about ¼ in. (6 mm) from the raw edge through the top layer only. Do the same with the bottom layer of fabric. Take out the basting stitches, then ask an adult to help you press the stitched edges flat.

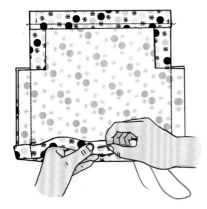

5 Fold the bottom edge of the dress over to the wrong side by ⅜ in. (1 cm) all the way around to make the hem, pin, and baste. Take out the pins, then machine stitch all the way around. Take out the basting stitches. Turn the dress right side out, then ask an adult to help you press the dress flat.

Pretty as a PICTURE!

6 Cut the ribbon in half. Attach the safety pin to one end of one ribbon, then push the pin through one of the channels at the top of the dress until it comes out at the other side. Remove the pin and push the other ribbon through the other channel in the same way. Put the dress on the doll, and tie the ribbons together in a bow at each shoulder, gathering up the fabric around her neck. Arrange the gathers neatly to look pretty.

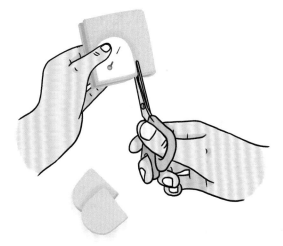

7 To make the shoes, trace the template on page 125 onto paper and cut out. Fold the felt square in half, pin the paper template to it, and cut out two shoe shapes neatly. Unpin the template, then use it to cut two more shoe shapes in the same way.

8 Pin two felt shoe shapes together and machine stitch them together around the curve, sewing about ⅜ in. (1 cm) from the felt edge. Take out the pins. Repeat this with the other two felt pieces. Trim the felt about ¼ in. (5 mm) from the stitch line, making sure you don't cut into the stitching.

9 Hand stitch a button onto each shoe (see page 117). If you push a small piece of card into the shoe first, it will stop you from stitching through to the back. Push the shoes onto the doll's feet.

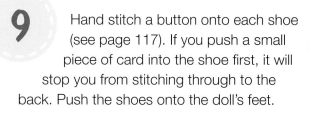

Teddy's picnic blanket

This is a perfect first project for getting you confident with your sewing machine. The blanket is just the thing for a teddy bears' picnic or perhaps as a pretty covering for a table in your room. Sew rick-rack around the edge to make a fancy border or simply turn the edges under and sew them in place for an even easier make.

You will need

At least 16-in. (40-cm) square of fabric

64 in. (160 cm) jumbo rick-rack

Contrasting thread for basting (tacking)

Sewing thread to match the fabric

Newspaper or brown wrapping paper for pattern

Pencil and ruler

Pinking shears

Pins

Sewing needle

Sewing machine

1 If your fabric needs to be cut to size, draw a 16-in. (40-cm) square on newspaper or brown wrapping paper and cut it out. (See page 112 for tips on cutting out squares and rectangles.) Pin this pattern to the fabric and cut it out.

2 Trim the edges of the fabric with the pinking shears so that the fabric will not fray as much.

3 Fold ⅜ in. (1 cm) over to the wrong side along one side of the fabric square and ask an adult to help you press it with an iron.

4 Fold the other three sides over in the same way and press with an iron again.

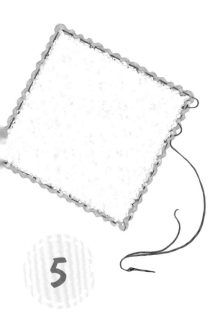

5

Turn the fabric over so that you're looking at the wrong side. Pin rick-rack around the edge of the fabric so that about half of it sticks out from the edge. Baste (tack) the rick-rack in place and take the pins out as you go.

Time for TEA!

6

Using the sewing machine, stitch the rick-rack in place, stitching about ¼ in. (5 mm) from the edge of the fabric. Remember to start and finish machine stitching securely (see page 114). Carefully take out the basting stitches.

Doll's quilt and pillow

If you've made the rag doll on page 92 or have a favorite teddy, then why not make this cute quilt and pillow to make sure he or she gets a good night's sleep?

You will need

For the quilt

16 x 18 in. (40 x 45 cm) patterned fabric (see page 112 for tips about cutting out squares and rectangles of fabric)

16 x 18 in. (40 x 45 cm) gingham fabric

16 x 18 in. (40 x 45 cm) cotton batting (wadding)

16 in. (40 cm) jumbo rick-rack, ¾ in. (2 cm) wide

For the pillow

10 x 7 in. (25 x 18 cm) patterned fabric

10 x 7 in. (25 x 18 cm) gingham fabric

10 x 7 in. (25 x 18 cm) cotton batting (wadding)

Sewing thread to match the patterned fabric

Pins

Sewing needle

Scissors

Sewing machine

Blunt pencil

Ruler

Tailor's chalk

Making the quilt

1 Place the patterned fabric right side up on the table. Pin the rick-rack along the top edge and then baste (tack) it in place, removing the pins as you go.

TIP

When you cut the fabric to the correct size, cut the gingham out first—that way you can use the squares to make sure you cut straight lines and right-angle corners. Then use the gingham as a pattern to cut around for the patterned fabric and wadding.

2 Put the gingham fabric right side down on top of the patterned fabric and then place the cotton batting (wadding) on top of the gingham. Pin and baste them together, then take out the pins. Make two marks with tailor's chalk about 4 in. (10 cm) apart on the bottom edge. These will show you where to begin and end stitching so that you remember to leave a gap.

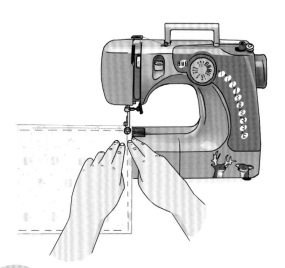

3 Machine stitch all around the quilt, stitching ⅝ in. (1.5 cm) from the edge along the sides and base and making sure that you stitch through the center of the rick-rack along the top edge. Remember to leave the gap at the bottom. Take out the basting stitches.

Cute BEDDING for your teddy

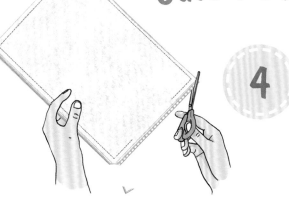

4 Snip the corners off with scissors, making sure that you do not cut into the stitches.

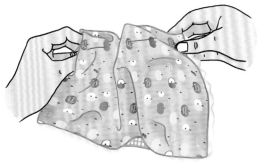

5 Turn the quilt the right way out by pushing the fabric through the gap. Push the corners out neatly using a blunt pencil.

doll's quilt and pillow **101**

6 Thread a needle, turn the seam allowance inside at the opening, and hand stitch the gap closed using small neat slipstitches (see page 113).

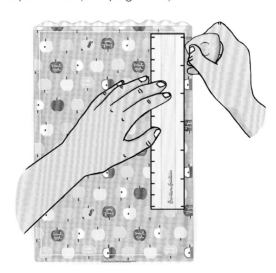

7 Using tailor's chalk and a ruler, draw a line all around the quilt 1 in. (2.5 cm) from the outer edge. Machine stitch along this line to hold all the layers together.

Making the pillow

1 Make the doll's pillow in exactly the same way as the quilt, but without the rick-rack—so miss out step 1.

Superbunny

Is it a plane? Is it a bird? No, it's Superbunny, ready to save the world. This cute toy would make a great gift for a younger brother or a friend ... but you won't ever want to give him away!

You will need

Templates on page 126

28 x 18 in. (70 x 45 cm) fleece fabric

18 x 2 in. (45 x 5 cm) red felt for the mask

14 x 8 in. (35 x 20 cm) blue gingham fabric for the cape (see page 112 for tips about cutting out squares and rectangles of fabric)

16 in. (40 cm) red ribbon, ⅞ in. (23 mm) wide, for the cape

12 in. (30 cm) blue ribbon, ⅝ in. (15 mm) wide, for the belt

Button, approx. ⅞ in. (22 mm) in diameter

Polyester toy filling

Sewing thread to match the fleece

Contrasting thread for basting (tacking)

Scissors

Sewing needle

Tailor's chalk

Sewing machine

Safety pin

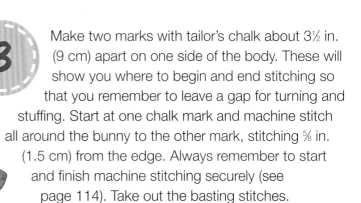

1 Ask an adult to photocopy the templates on page 126 using the 200% zoom on the photocopier. Cut out the bunny body pattern and the mask pattern. Fold the fleece in half and pin the bunny paper pattern to both layers so that, when you cut it out, you have two bunny pieces.

2 Put the bunny shapes together with right sides together and pin all the way around. Baste (tack) all the way around, taking out the pins as you go.

3 Make two marks with tailor's chalk about 3½ in. (9 cm) apart on one side of the body. These will show you where to begin and end stitching so that you remember to leave a gap for turning and stuffing. Start at one chalk mark and machine stitch all around the bunny to the other mark, stitching ⅝ in. (1.5 cm) from the edge. Always remember to start and finish machine stitching securely (see page 114). Take out the basting stitches.

4 Using the tips of sharp scissors, make small snips from the edge of the fabric in toward the stitching, being careful not to cut into the stitches. Make the snips all around the curves of the ears, arms, and feet so that the finished rabbit will be a nice rounded shape. Make a snip between the legs, between the ears, and under the arms as well.

5 Turn the bunny the right way out, pushing the arms, legs, and ears out with the blunt end of a pencil. Push small pieces of toy filling inside the bunny, making sure that you push it right up into the legs, arms, and ears. Use the pencil to help with this.

6 When the bunny is well stuffed, thread a needle, then turn the fleece seam allowance inside at the opening and slipstitch (see page 113) the opening closed. Start and finish with a few small stitches to secure the thread.

7 To make the cape, lay the rectangle of gingham fabric on the table with a long side at the top. Fold over the top edge by 1¼ in. (3 cm) and pin. Baste, taking out the pins as you go. Machine stitch, sewing ¾ in. (2 cm) from the folded top edge. Take out the basting stitches.

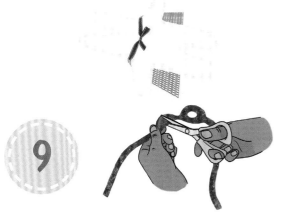

8 Fasten a safety pin to one end of the ribbon for the cape and push it through the channel you have just made across the top of the cape until it comes out of the other side. Take out the safety pin and tie the cape around the bunny's neck, fastening it in place with a knot in the ribbon.

9 Cut the eyes out of the mask pattern by making a fold in the paper where each eye is and cutting a slit — then you can cut the eye shape out carefully. Pin the mask pattern to the red felt. Draw around the inside of the eye holes with a pencil. Cut out the mask and then cut out the eyes, by folding the felt in the same way as you did for the paper.

10 To make the belt, wrap the ribbon around the bunny's tummy and hand sew it in place with a few stitches. Overlap the ends of the ribbon for a snug fit.

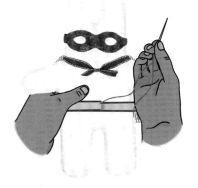

11 To finish, stitch a button onto the belt (see page 117). Now he's ready to fly!

Patchwork checkerboard ☺☺○

This colorful patchwork mat doubles up as a games board for playing tic-tac-toe (noughts and crosses). To play the game, use buttons in two colors or discs of felt or card. Take turns to put a counter down to try to make a line of three.

You will need

11-in. (28-cm) square of gingham fabric

17 x 12 in. (43 x 25 cm) patterned fabric (see page 112 for tips about cutting out squares and rectangles of fabric)

13-in. (33-cm) square of backing fabric

Contrasting thread for basting (tacking)

Sewing thread to match the fabric

Scrap paper (squared is easiest), ruler, and pencil

Pins

Scissors

Sewing needle

Sewing machine

TIP
See page 112 for tips about cutting out squares and rectangles of fabric.

1 Draw a square measuring 5 in. (12 cm) on paper and cut it out. Fold the gingham fabric in half. Pin the paper pattern onto the fabric and cut around it to make two squares. Take off the pattern, pin it to the folded gingham again and cut two more squares to make four altogether; make sure you line up the edges of the pattern with the squares of the gingham. Now do the same with the patterned fabric and then cut out one more square so that you have five patterned squares.

2 Take one patterned square and one gingham square. Lay them on top of each other with right sides together. Pin along one side and baste (tack), taking out the pins as you go. Machine stitch in place, then take out the basting stitches. Always remember to start and finish machine stitching securely (see page 114). Try to keep a seam allowance of ⅝ in. (1.5 cm) for all your seams in this project so that the squares stay nice and square!

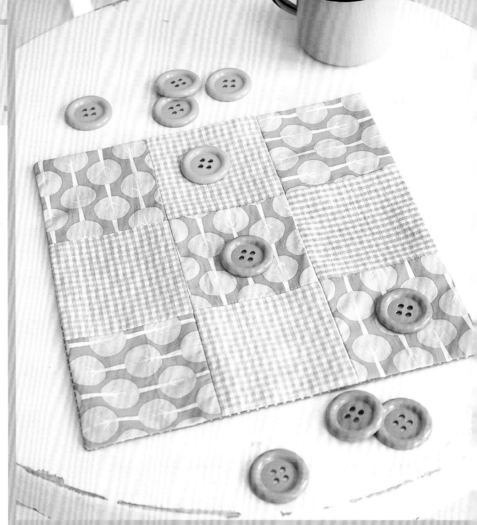

3 Pin another patterned square to the other side of the gingham square, with right sides together again. Baste and stitch in the same way as before to make a strip of three.

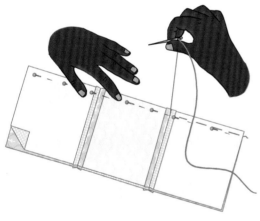

4 Now make another strip of three squares, but as the first one was "pattern, gingham, pattern," this one needs to be "gingham, pattern, gingham." Ask an adult to help you press the seams of both strips open on the wrong side. Then, with right sides together, pin the two strips together. Baste, take out the pins, and machine stitch. Then take out the basting stitches.

5 Use the remaining three squares to make a third strip like the first (pattern, gingham, pattern). Ask an adult to help you press the seams open and then pin this to the other strips (be careful to pin to the correct side so it makes a checkerboard pattern). Baste and machine stitch them together as before. Ask an adult to help you press the long seams open.

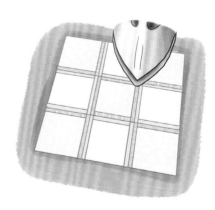

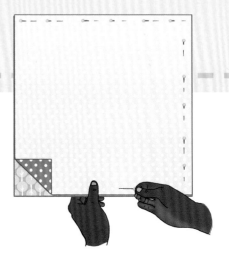

6 Take the backing fabric and place it on top of the patchwork panel with right sides together. Pin all the way around and then baste, taking out the pins as you go. If the backing fabric is a bit bigger than the patchwork, carefully cut off the extra bits so that the two pieces are level.

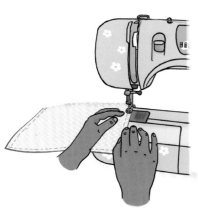

7 Make two marks with tailor's chalk about 3 in. (8 cm) apart along one side. These will show you where to begin and end stitching so that you remember to leave a gap for turning. Start at one mark and machine stitch all around to the other mark, stitching ⅝ in. (1.5 cm) from the edge. Take out the basting stitches.

8 Snip the corners off with scissors, making sure that you do not cut into the stitching. This will help the board to lie flat. Turn the panel the right way out, through the gap, pushing the corners out with the end of a pencil.

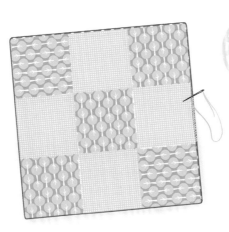

9 Thread a needle, turn the seam allowance inside at the opening, and hand stitch the opening closed with small, neat, slipstitches (see page 113) starting and finishing with a few small stitches to secure the thread. Ask an adult to help you press the board game flat, find or make some counters, and you are ready to play!

Scooter bag

This funky bag is the perfect way to accessorize your scooter and create a handy holder for bits and pieces. You can design your own funny face, too, using scraps of felt and buttons.

You will need

Templates on page 127

26 x 8 in. (65 x 20 cm) red felt (see page 112 for tips about cutting out squares and rectangles of fabric)

10 x 5 in. (25 x 12 cm) turquoise felt

5 x 3 in. (12 x 8 cm) green felt

6-in. (15-cm) square of yellow felt

7 x 4 in. (18 x 10 cm) white felt

Two odd buttons for eyes

40 in. (100 cm) ribbon, ¾ in. (2 cm) wide

Contrasting thread for basting (tacking)

Embroidery floss (thread) to match the buttons

Sewing thread to match buttons

Red and turquoise sewing threads

Tracing paper, scrap paper, and pencil

Pins

Scissors

Embroidery and sewing needles

Sewing machine

Two safety pins

1 Measure and cut an 8 x 6-in. (20 x 15-cm) rectangle of red felt for the front, an 8 x 6¾-in. (20 x 17.5-cm) piece of red felt for the back, and three 8 x 1¼-in. (20 x 3-cm) strips of turquoise felt for the stripes. Now photocopy the templates on page 127 or trace them onto scrap paper, then cut them out. Pin them onto the right color of felt, and draw around them. Cut two red flaps, two green eyes, two yellow ears, and one set of white teeth. Take out the pins and remove the paper patterns.

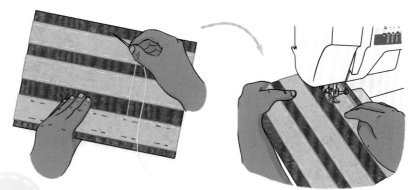

2 Lay the front of the bag (the smaller rectangle) on your table with the long side at the top. Pin the stripes across the rectangle and baste (tack) them in place, taking the pins out as you go. Don't worry about measuring the distance between the stripes: it doesn't matter if they look a bit wonky. Machine stitch the stripes in place, sewing about ¼ in. (5 mm) from each side. Always remember to start and finish machine stitching securely (see page 114). You do not need to stitch along the ends of the stripes.

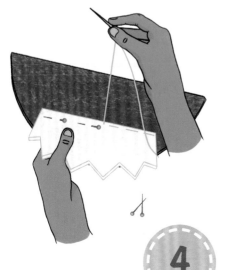

3 Pin the felt teeth onto the curved edge of one of the flap pieces, so that the pointy teeth stick out over the edge. Baste them in place, removing the pins as you go.

4 Thread a needle with a length of embroidery floss (thread) and tie a knot in the end. Pin the green felt eyes onto the second flap piece. Sewing from the back to the front of the felt, sew a line of running stitches around both eyes and finish on the back with another knot. Take out the pins.

5 Thread a sewing needle with sewing thread and sew the buttons onto the green felt eyes (see page 117), starting and finishing with a few small stitches on the back. Stitch the buttons on wonkily for a googly-eyed look!

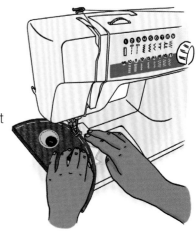

6 Put the flap piece with the teeth, teeth side up, on your table, then place the other flap piece, eye side up, on top. Pin the pieces together around the curved edge. Baste around the edge, take the pins out, and machine stitch about ¼ in. (5 mm) from the edge. Take the basting stitches out from around the curve and also the ones that held the teeth in place.

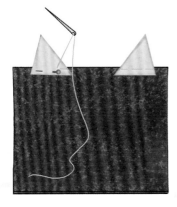

7 Take the back of the bag (the larger rectangle) and pin the ears to the top of it. (Measure the felt if you're not sure which is which: the top and bottom edges are longer than the sides.) Baste the ears in place.

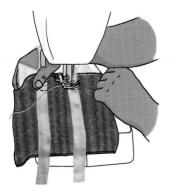

TIP

For tips on how to sew on a ribbon without basting first, see page 116.

8 Turn the back piece over. Cut the ribbon in half. Fold one piece in half again to find the center. Pin the center of the ribbon 2½ in. (6 cm) from one side and ⅝ in. (1.5 cm) from the top edge. Do the same with the other piece of ribbon on the other side. Baste the ribbons in place and then take out the pins. Machine stitch the ribbons, using the reverse on the machine to stitch backward and forward a few times to hold the ribbons securely.

9 Pin the ribbon ends to the middle of the felt with safety pins to keep them out of the way when you sew the bag together.

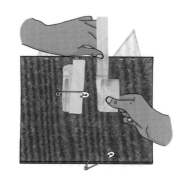

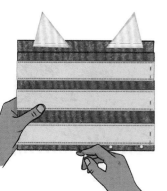

10 Place the back piece, ears side up, on the table. Pin the stripy front piece to this, stripy side up, so the bottom and side edges line up (the top of the back piece will be a bit higher than the front). Baste around the sides and the bottom, taking out the pins as you go.

11 Pin the flap on top of the bag, eye side up, lining up the top of the flap with the top of the back piece of the bag. Baste across the top, taking out the pins as you go. Machine stitch all the way around the bag and then take out all the basting stitches. Use the ribbons to tie your pouch to the front of your scooter or bike. The flap will keep the bag closed and your bits and pieces safe.

Techniques

All the sewing techniques in this book are easy to learn and this section shows you everything you need to know to make the projects and many more of your own. Read them carefully before you start to use your machine. Asking an adult who sews is a great idea, too, as they will have lots of handy tips to pass on to you.

Using a pattern

There are lots of templates in this book to help you make patterns for the projects. To use them:

Trace the template onto tracing paper or thin paper that you can see through, and cut it out to make a pattern.

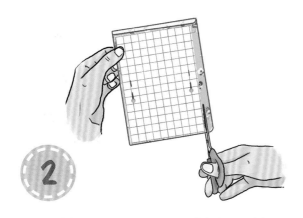

Pin this pattern onto your fabric, making sure that the pattern is flat with no creases. Position the pattern close to the edges of the fabric so that you don't waste any. Try to pin patterns, especially rectangles, in line with the tiny threads you can see in the fabric (on felt it doesn't matter). Cut around the pattern with sharp scissors, then take out the pins and remove the pattern.

How to use half-size templates

Some of the templates on pages 118–127 need to be doubled in size to make the pattern big enough. Ask somebody to photocopy the template for you, using the 200% zoom button on the photocopier.

Square or rectangular templates

- Many of the projects start with a square or rectangular pattern. To cut these out, make a paper pattern first.
- For small squares and rectangles, it is easiest to draw these on squared paper—that way, you can be sure that all your angles are right-angles.
- For large squares that won't fit on the squared paper, mark the length of the sides on a corner of a large sheet of newspaper or brown wrapping paper. Join up the two marks to make a triangle. Fold the triangle over along this line and cut around it; that will give you a perfect square.
- For large rectangles, you will need to use a set square to draw the right angles. Carefully check the lengths of each side when you have drawn them to make sure that opposite sides are equal.

Basting (tacking)

If you sew across pins with a sewing machine, the machine needle may break, so the best way to hold fabrics together before you machine stitch is to pin them together first and then baste (tack).

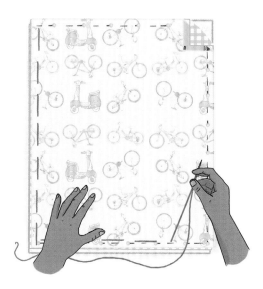

1 Thread a needle with brightly colored sewing thread that's a different color to the fabric, so that you can see your stitches easily. Sew the fabric together with big, straight stitches, then take out the pins. Now your fabric is ready to be machine stitched!

2 After you've finished machine stitching, take out the basting stitches: just cut the basting thread and use a pin or your fingers to pull out the basting stitches.

Slipstitch

This stitch is used to sew two layers of fabric together with stitches that show at the edges. It is also useful to close up a gap after stuffing an object such as the Superbunny on page 103.

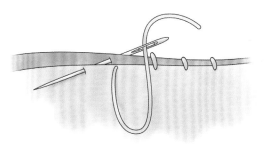

Begin with a knot or a few small stitches at the back of the two layers. Push the needle through both layers to the front, ⅛ in. (2–3 mm) from the edge, and pull the thread right through. Take the needle over the top of both layers to the back again and push it through to the front a little way along the seam. The stitches go over the edges of the two fabrics. Finish with a knot or a few small stitches.

Using a sewing machine

Once you have got your sewing machine, then follow the manufacturer's instructions carefully so that you can thread it and work out the correct tension confidently. Always test out your stitches on scrap fabric before you begin so that you can alter the tension or stitch length if you have to.

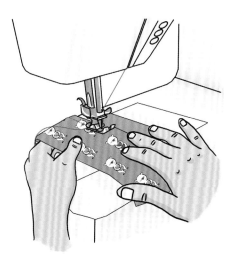

1 Ask an adult to help you prepare the bobbin and thread the machine with the sewing thread for your project.

2 Check that you have selected a straight stitch in the correct size.

3 Raise the presser foot and the needle and place your fabric underneath. The machine plate on your sewing machine should have width markings that you can use as your guide for your seam allowances. Line up the edge of your fabric with one of the lines; depending on the size you want your seam allowance to be, this will be either ⅜ in. (1cm) or ⅝ in. (1.5 cm).

4 Lower the presser foot and start to stitch by pressing on the foot pedal. After a few stitches, press the reverse stitch button on your machine and stitch a few stitches backward and then forward again. This will secure the stitching.

5 To keep your seam straight, keep the edge of the fabric lined up with the line on the machine plate. Gently guide the fabric away from you with one hand at the front, and hold the fabric as it moves out at the back. Make sure that you keep your fingers well away from the needle when you have your foot on the pedal! Don't pull the fabric, as the machine will do the work for you and will keep the fabric moving—you just need to keep it in a straight line.

6 When you come to the end, select the reverse stitch button again and stitch a few stitches backward and forward to secure the thread. Now check that the needle is out of the fabric. If it is not, use the wheel at the side of the machine to raise it, then raise the presser foot and pull the fabric away with the threads still attached. Cut the threads about 4 in. (10 cm) from the needle. You have now stitched a seam!

Turning corners

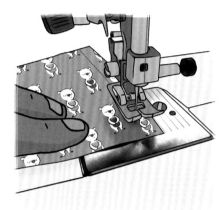

1 To turn a corner when stitching, machine stitch in a straight line to the corner point of the seam allowance and stop stitching. If the needle is not in the fabric, turn the wheel at the side to lower it into the fabric.

2 Lift the presser foot up and swivel the fabric around so that the edge that you need to stitch lines up with the line on the machine plate as before. Put the presser foot down again and begin stitching along the fabric, using the same seam allowance.

Undoing machine stitching when you have gone wrong

Often when using a sewing machine, you may find that you have stitched the wrong pieces of fabric together, or stitched across the seam allowance when you didn't mean to. If this happens, simply remove the fabric from the machine (see opposite).

Using a seam ripper, push the pointed end up through the stitches that you want to take out and cut it with the sharp edge. Repeat this along the stitching line, then pull the threads out of the fabric to neaten it.

Measurements

Measurements are given in both inches and centimeters (or millimeters) for all projects, but choose which you want to use and stick to it for the whole project. Don't try to mix them or pieces may not fit together properly!

Stitching on ribbons without basting (tacking)

It is important never to machine stitch over pins because the needle can hit a pin, break, and fly into your eye. However, sometimes basting is a nuisance when sewing on pieces of ribbon. This is a way to sew on ribbons without basting.

Pressing seams open

Often when you have stitched a seam, you will need to press it open.

Pin the ribbon in place and put it under the presser foot of the sewing machine. Use the wheel at the side to lower the needle until it goes right through the ribbon and the fabric, holding them securely. Take out the pin. Sew the ribbon in place using the reverse stitch on the machine to go backward and forward a few times so that the ribbon is held in place firmly.

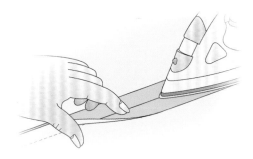

Ask an adult to help you do this. Run the tip of the iron along the seam on the wrong side, so that the two edges of fabric open up to lie flat on either side of the seam.

Sewing on buttons

You can use buttons as decorations, as in the eyes on the Scooter Bag on page 109, and to hold things closed, as in the Needle Case on page 86.

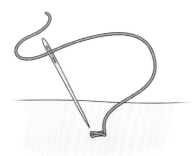

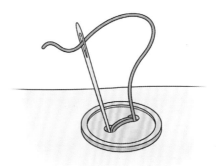

1 Mark the place where you want the button to go. Push the needle up from the back of the fabric and sew a few stitches over and over in this place.

2 Now bring the needle up through one of the holes in the button. Push the needle back down through the second hole and through the fabric. Bring it back up through the first hole. Repeat this five or six times. If there are four holes in the button, use all four of them to make a cross pattern. Make sure that you keep the stitches close together under the middle of the button.

3 Finish with a few small stitches over and over on the back of the fabric and trim the thread.

Templates

All the templates provided here are full size, except for the superbunny, laundry bag, and rag doll body, which are half size. Full size templates can be photocopied or traced as they are. The half-size templates need to be doubled in size (see page 112).

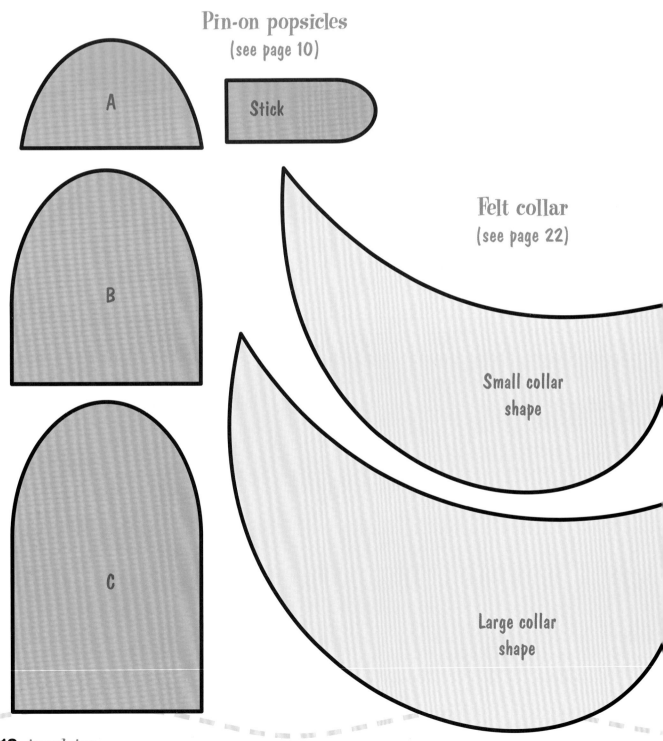

Pin-on popsicles
(see page 10)

A

Stick

B

C

Felt collar
(see page 22)

Small collar
shape

Large collar
shape

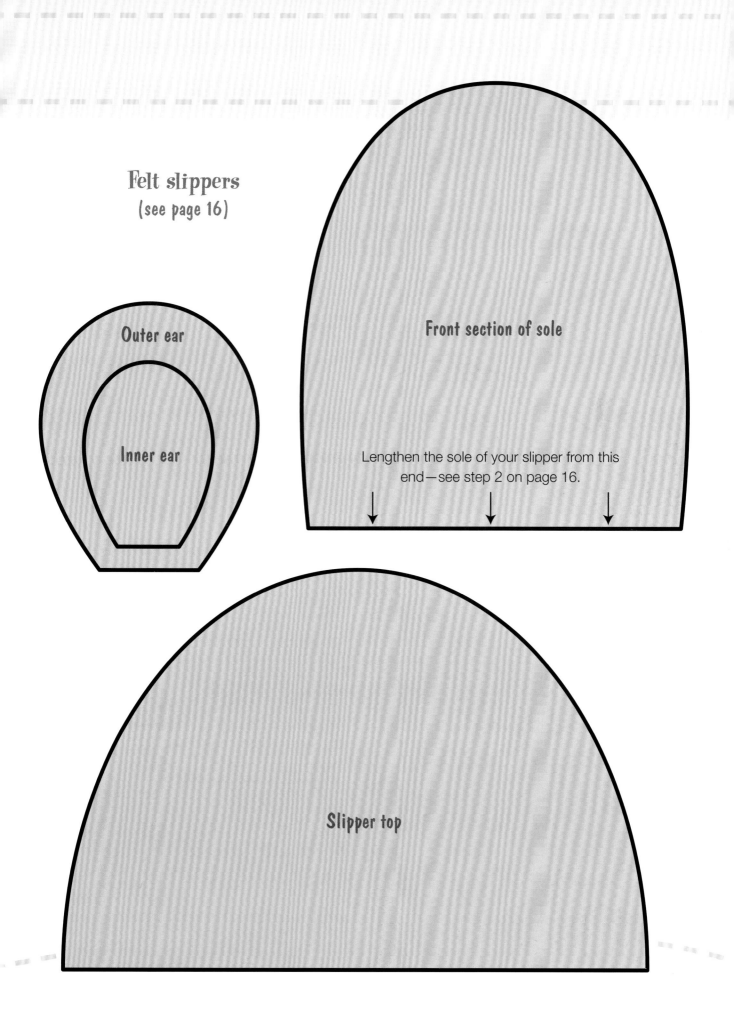

Felt slippers
(see page 16)

Outer ear

Inner ear

Front section of sole

Lengthen the sole of your slipper from this end—see step 2 on page 16.

Slipper top

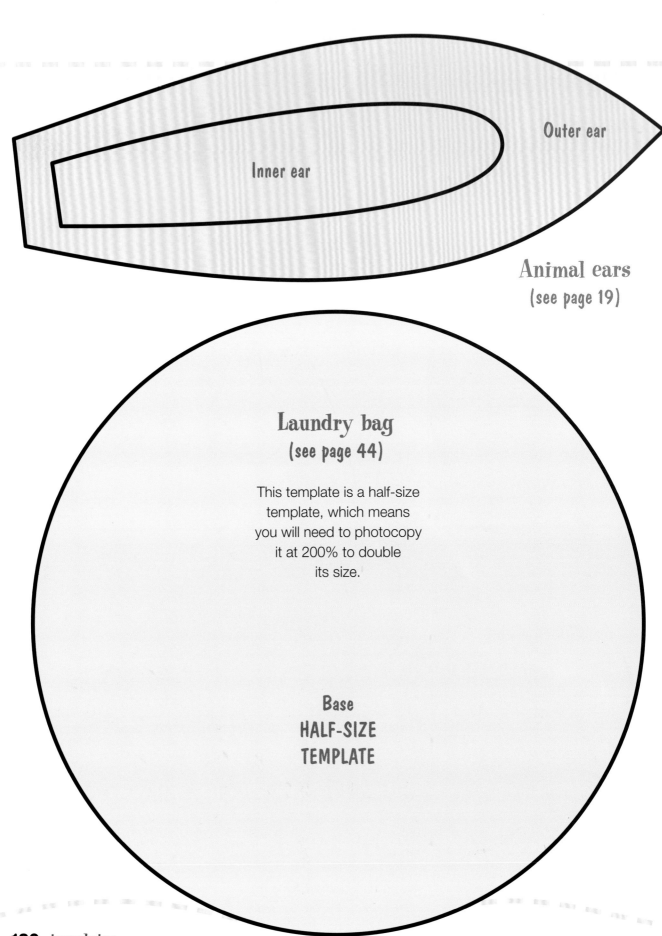

Outer ear

Inner ear

Animal ears
(see page 19)

Laundry bag
(see page 44)

This template is a half-size
template, which means
you will need to photocopy
it at 200% to double
its size.

**Base
HALF-SIZE
TEMPLATE**

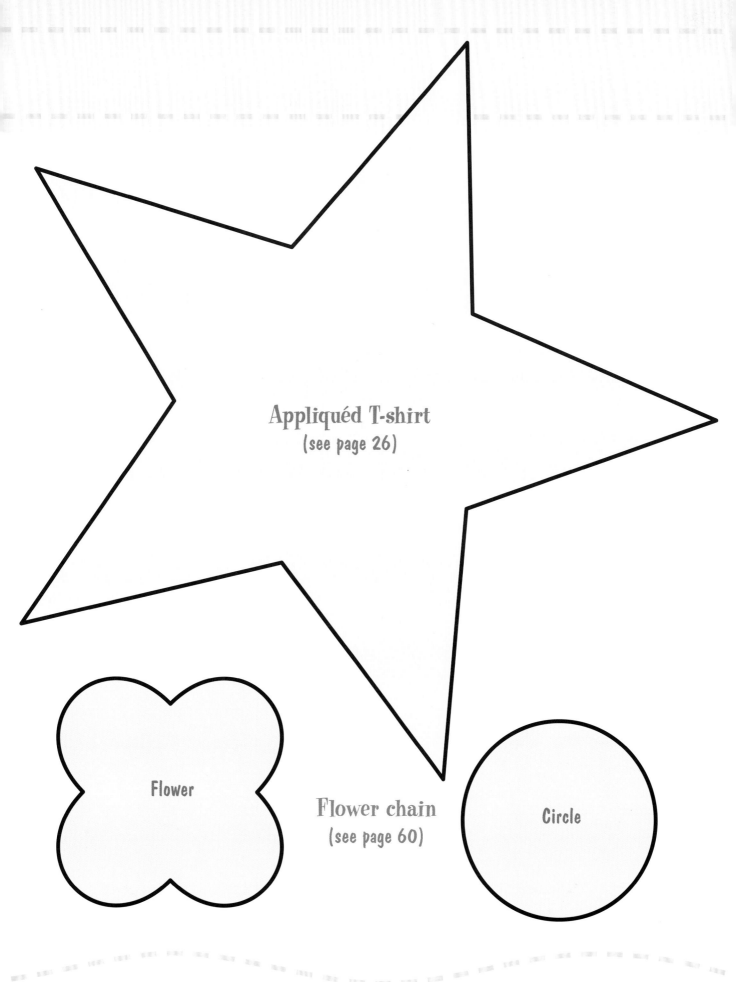

Appliquéd T-shirt
(see page 26)

Flower

Flower chain
(see page 60)

Circle

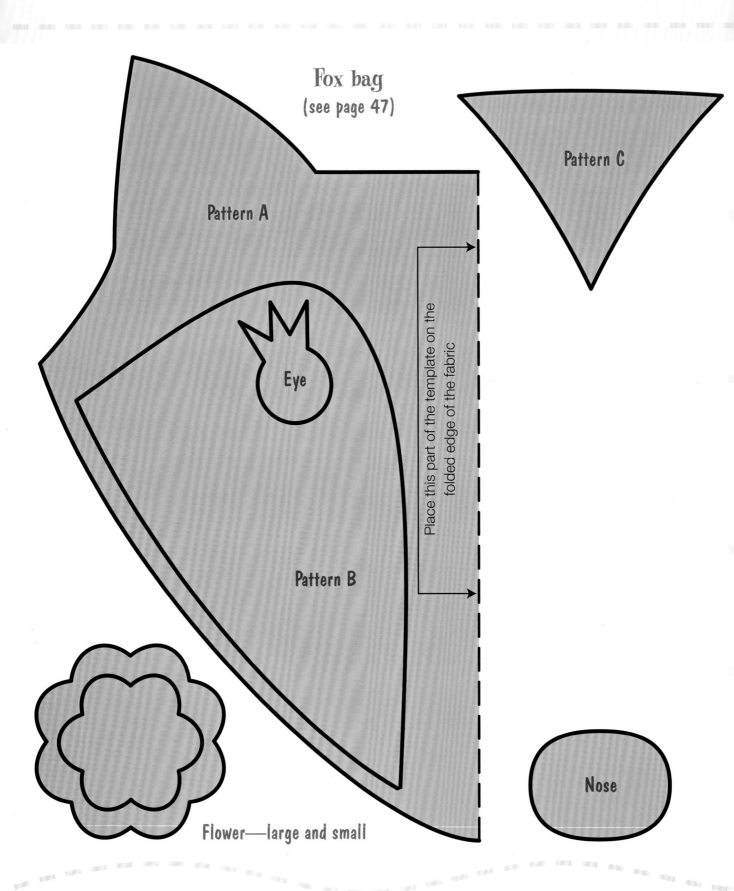

Fox bag
(see page 47)

Pattern A

Pattern C

Eye

Place this part of the template on the folded edge of the fabric

Pattern B

Nose

Flower—large and small

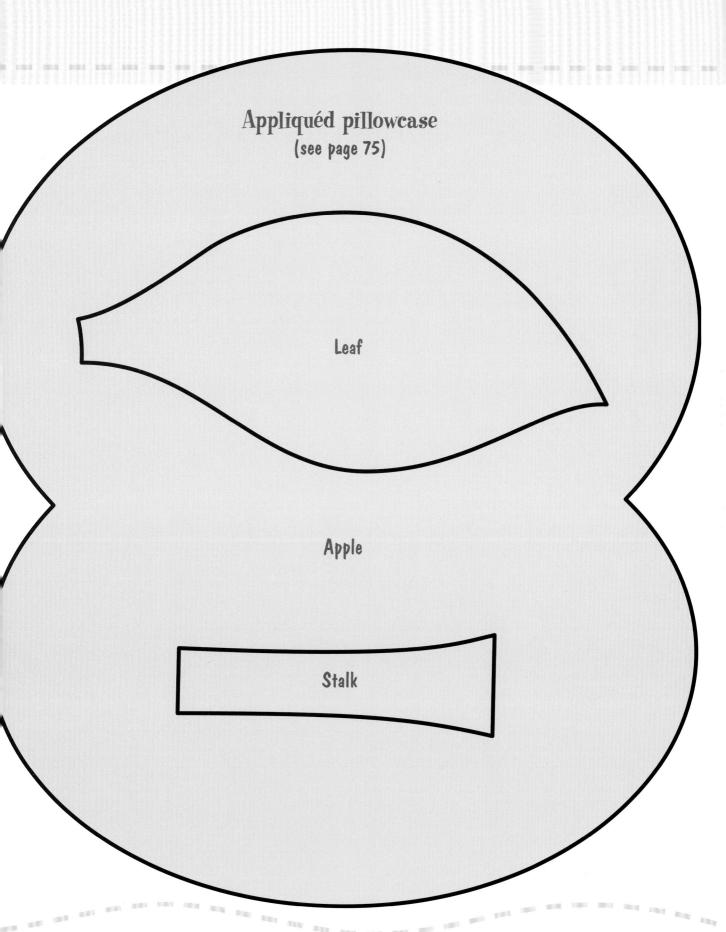

Appliquéd pillowcase
(see page 75)

Leaf

Apple

Stalk

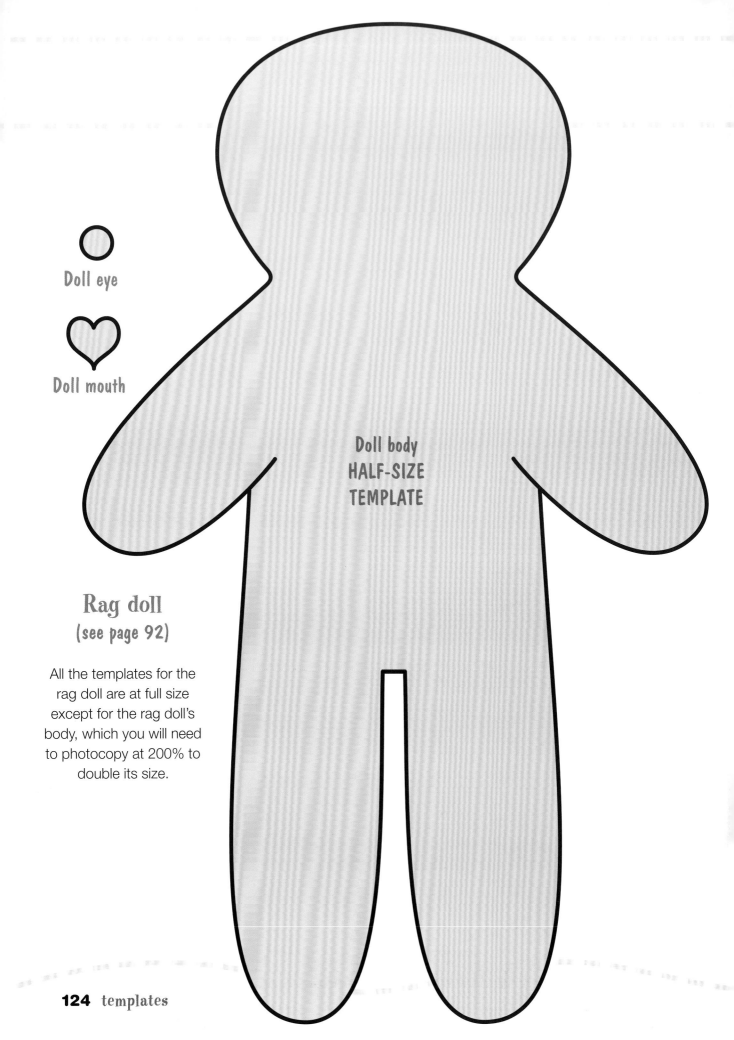

Doll eye

Doll mouth

Doll body
HALF-SIZE
TEMPLATE

Rag doll
(see page 92)

All the templates for the
rag doll are at full size
except for the rag doll's
body, which you will need
to photocopy at 200% to
double its size.

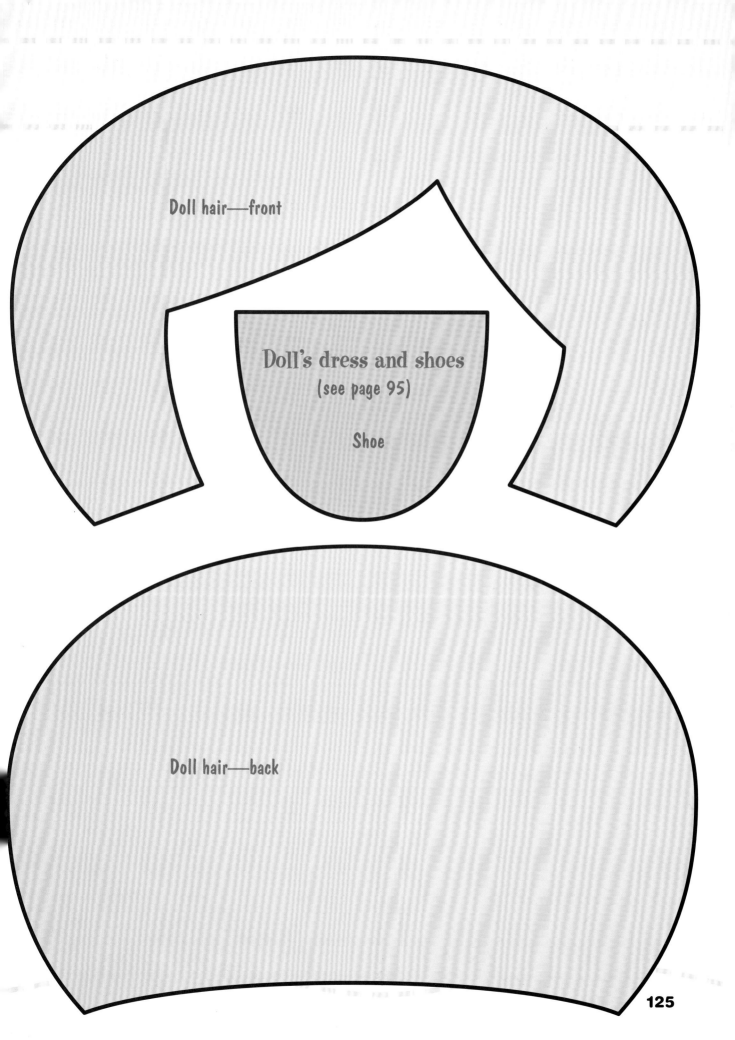

Doll hair—front

Doll's dress and shoes
(see page 95)

Shoe

Doll hair—back

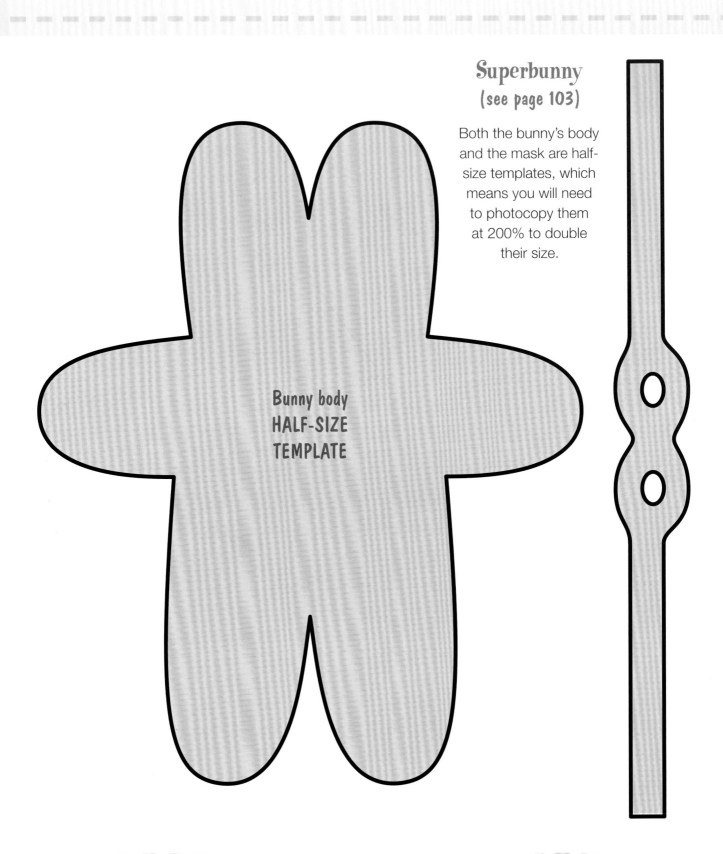

Superbunny
(see page 103)

Both the bunny's body and the mask are half-size templates, which means you will need to photocopy them at 200% to double their size.

Bunny body
HALF-SIZE
TEMPLATE

Scooter bag
(see page 109)

Eye 1

Eye 2

Ear

Teeth

Flap

Index

Suppliers

US

A C Moore
www.acmoore.com

Create For Less
www.createforless.com

Hobby Lobby
www.hobbylobby.com

Jo-ann Fabric & Crafts
www.joann.com

Michaels
www.michaels.com

UK

Buttonbag
www.buttonbag.co.uk

Early Learning Centre
www.elc.co.uk

Homecrafts Direct
www.homecrafts.co.uk

Hobbycraft
www.hobbycraft.co.uk

John Lewis
www.johnlewis.co.uk

Acknowledgments

Many thanks to Debbie Patterson for her beautiful photography and sparkling personality, Sarah Hogget for calmly and graciously making sense of it all, and Susan Akass for checking it all so meticulously. Thank you to Rachel Boulton for the illustrations and Barbara Zuñiga for the design of the book. Thank you also to Sally Powell, Fahema Khanam, and Carmel Edmonds at CICO Books for help and support throughout and to Cindy Richards at CICO Books for commissioning the book in the first place. Thank you, thank you all!

FEB 2 8 2017